馬上說
生活英文
迷你短句

Sentences

國家圖書館出版品預行編目資料

馬上說，生活英文迷你短句 / 雅典英研所編著
-- 初版 -- 新北市：雅典文化，民110.12
面；　公分. --（全民學英文；62）
ISBN 978-626-95008-5-7（平裝）
1. 英語　　2. 會話
805.188　　　　　　　　　　　　110017576

全民學英文系列 62

馬上說，生活英文迷你短句

編著／雅典英研所
責任編輯／張文娟
美術編輯／鄭孝儀
封面設計／林鈺恆

法律顧問：方圓法律事務所／涂成樞律師

總經銷：永續圖書有限公司
永續圖書線上購物網

www.foreverbooks.com.tw

出版日／2021年12月

雅典文化

出版社

22103　新北市汐止區大同路三段194號9樓之1
TEL　（02）8647-3663
FAX　（02）8647-3660

序言

您有學了很久英文卻還是無法應用的困擾嗎？

從學校學了好多文法，背了一堆單字，但遇到該開口時卻一個字一句話都開不了口嗎？

本書由最簡單的問候 How are you doing? 開啟您的對話，輕鬆簡短又道地，不需要超強的英文能力及高分的考試成績一樣可以運用自如。

學語言最重要的就是運用，除了學校正規的語言教學之外，您還必須必備像這樣的口袋生活工具書，告訴您學校沒有教的超實用生活短句。

從人與人基本的日常生活對話、電話禮儀、到吃飯、看電影等等，一次提供給您在一天的生活中有機會應用到的英文句子，讓您走到哪講到哪。

馬上說 生活英文
Say it now
迷你短句

PART2
家人

PART 3
朋友

PART4
情人

PART 5
學校

PART6
電話

PART 7
吃飯

PART 8
娛樂

PART 9
交通工具搭乘

Chapter 1

問候招呼與回答

🎧 track 001

你好嗎 (第一次見面)

How do you do?

解 析

就像 How are you? 一樣，是你好的意思，
只限於第一次見面使用。

會 話

例 How do you do? (shake hands)
你好。

例 How do you do.
你好。

小·叮·嚀

要注意的是，當對方如果先開口說 How
do you do? 的時候，回答一定只有 How
do you do. 沒有其它回答。當然，在第二
次見面之後就不需要再使用這句話了。

很高興認識你

Nice to meet you.

解析

可能會在第一次見面寒喧完說出口，也可能是在對話與會面結束要分開的時候說。當然如果想要加強語氣，也可以說：It's so nice to meet you.

會話 1

例 Hi, I'm Annie.

嗨，我是安妮。

例 Hi, I'm Ben, nice to meet you.

嗨，我是班，很高興認識你。

例 Nice to meet you, too.

很高興認識你。

會話 2

例 Ok, I hope I'll see you soon. It was nice to meet you.

希望下次再見面，很高興認識你。

例 Yeah, same here.

我也是。

小·叮·嚀

如果是巧遇朋友，千萬不能這樣說哦，要改成：Nice to see you.

🎧 track 002

你好嗎

How are you doing?

解析

最常使用的就是 How are you doing? 如果在看英文電影或是影集時，一定會常常聽到他們遇到朋友開口的第一句話就是：Hey, how are you doing?

會話 （速食店櫃台）

例 How are you doing today? What would you like to have?

嗨，你好，今天想吃點什麼？

例 Uhhh, can I have a cheese burger without tomato?

呃，可以給我一個不加蕃茄的起士漢堡嗎？

迷你短句

例 Sure.

沒問題。

小·叮·嚀

> 此外，這句話也是有 Hi! 或是 Hello! 的
> 意思，所以如果你問對方這句話的時候，
> 對方沒有回答也是很正常的哦！

下次見

Later, gator!

解 析

這句話其實就等同於 See you later! 這裡
的 gator 指的是 alligator，意思是鱷魚，沒
有什麼特別的意思，只是美國人習慣用的
俏皮說法。

會 話 1

例 Well, I think I need to go, see you!

好吧，我該走了，下次見。

例 Later, gator!

下次見囉。

會話2

例 Don't you have a class now?

你不是應該要去上課了嗎？

例 Oh right, see you!

對啊，待會見了。

小·叮·嚀

用 See you later!, Later! 或是 See you!也
可以。

🎧track 003

很高興又見面了

Nice to see you!

解 析

不同於 Nice to mcct you，這句話可用於
已經認識的朋友，再度見面時表達的開心
之情。

會 話

例 Is that Catherine?

那不是凱瑟琳嗎？

例 Yeah, I think that's her.

好像是她耶。

例 I think I should go say hi.

我想過去打聲招呼。

例 Sure!

去吧！

例 Hey! Catherine! Nice to see you here!

嘿！凱瑟琳！真高興在這裡見到你！

例 Annie! Nice to see you too!

安妮！我也很開心見到你！

最近過得如何？

How have you been?

解析

對於久沒見面的朋友，打招呼時可以順便問一下他最近過的怎麼樣。

會話1

例 Sweetie, how have you been?

親愛的你最近過得如何？

例 I'm doing just fine, thank you, what about you?

我過得還可以啦,謝謝你,那你呢?

例 I'm all right.

還好啊。

會話 2

例 I wonder how he has been lately.

不知道他最近過得如何。

例 Why don't you call him?

你可以打給他啊?

 🎧 track 004

好久不見
It's been a long time!

解析

也可以說 Long time no see! 同樣都是好久不見的意思。

會話 1

例 Hi! I didn't know you are coming too! It's been a long time!

嗨!我怎麼不知道你也會來!好久不見!

迷你短句

例 I'm so glad to see you here!
在這裡見到你真是太開心了！

會話 2

例 Hey, long time no see.
嘿，好久不見。

例 Yeah, it's been a long time.
對啊，好久不見。

例 You look great.
你看起來過得很好。

你最近跑去哪了啊？
Where have you been lately?

解析

也屬於好久不見的招呼語，用在較熟的朋友比較洽當。

會話 1

例 Why didn't you answer my phone call?
Where have you been lately?
你為什麼不回我電話，你最近去哪了啊？

例 I'm sorry. I've been pretty busy lately.
對不起，我最近很忙。

例 At least you can text me back!
至少可以回傳個簡訊吧！

會話2

例 Where have you been? I've been looking for you!
你去哪裡了啊，我一直在找你！

例 I was on a business trip in Japan. I thought I had told you.
我去日本出差啊，我以為我跟你說過了。

例 I don't think so.
你沒有。

🎧 track 005

你(最近)在幹嘛？

What are you up to?

解析

問朋友最近都在忙些什麼，或是也可以當作朋友聊天的開場白，看對方現在在做什麼。

會 話

例 Hey, it's been a long time. What are you up to?

嘿好久不見，最近在幹嘛？

例 I've been preparing for the midterm, and it's killing me.

我在準備期中考啊，累死我了。

小·叮·嚀

> 有時候有些人都會懶惰而省略 are 而說成 What you up to? 也是一樣的意思哦。

希望下次再見

Hope to see you again!

解 析

除了道別說的 See you! 或是 Bye，還可以告訴對方希望下次再見，也可以說成 Hope to see you soon.

會 話 1

例 Thank you for inviting me today.

謝謝你今天邀請我來。

例 No problem. Hope to see you again.
　不用客氣，希望下次再見。

會話 2

例 Hey, I need to go, nice party.
　嘿我要走了，很棒的派對。

例 See you soon!
　下次見！

我也是/彼此彼此
Same here.

解 析

當回答別人的時候，除了用 Me too. 、So do I. 之外也可以説 Same here. 表示你跟對方一樣也這麼覺得。

會話 1

例 I'm so glad to meet you.
　非常高興認識你。

例 Same here.
　彼此彼此。

會話 2

例 All right, I have to go, bed time.
好了我要走了,該睡了。

例 Same here.
我也是。

例 Good night.
晚安。

很高興跟你談話
Nice talking to you!

解析

在與對方結束對話的最後,就可以說這句話以表達很高興見面及談話的禮貌。

會話 1

例 It was nice talking to you!
很高興跟你談話!

例 You too.
我也是。

會話 2

例 Nice talking to you.
很高興與你談話。

例 Same here, see you soon.
我也是,下次見。

小·叮·嚀

> 這裡回答的 You too, 是 Nice talking to
> you, too. 的簡略說法,所以聽到別人不是
> 說 Me too. 也別覺得奇怪哦。

track 007

好好玩

Have fun!

解 析

在得知對方即將去玩或是做一件有趣的事
就可以說Have fun! 有時候也有開玩笑挖
苦對方的意思。

會話 1

例 My plane to England leaves in three
hours, I have to go now!

我去英國的飛機再小三時就要起飛了,我得走了!

例 Have fun!
好好玩啊!

例 Thank you. I will!
謝謝,我會的!

會話 2

例 I can't believe I have to take the night shift five days in a row!
我不敢相信我竟然連續五天要值班!

例 Well, what can I say? Have fun!
那你就好好享受吧!

祝你有個美好的一天
Have a good/nice day!

解 析

在早上或是中午與人交談到尾聲時,可以用祝福對方有個美好的一天當作結束。

例 Hi, Mrs. Lee! Are you taking your kids to school?

嗨,李太太,你要帶小孩去上學了啊?

例 Good morning, Mrs. Wu. Yes, and we are so late!

早安!吳太太。沒錯,而且我們已經遲到了!

例 Ok, you had better hurry up! Have a nice day!

好好,那你們趕快去吧!祝你有個美好的一天!

🎧 track 008

祝你有個美好的週末

Have a nice weekend!

在星期五星期六都可以這麼說,祝福對方有一個美好的週末;也可以將 weekend 改成 week 或是 trip.

迷你短句

會話 1

例 See you next week!
下週見！

例 Have a nice weekend!
祝你有個美好的週末

例 You too.
你也是。

會話 2

例 How long are you going this time for the business trip?
你這次出差要去多久？

例 A week from this Wednesday.
整整一個禮拜。

例 Hope you have a good trip.
希望旅途順利。

我過得還不錯

I am doing good.

解析

回答我很好時有很多種回答，除了I'm fine,
I'm ok等，也可以用這句話表示。

會話 1

例 How are you?

你好嗎？

例 I am doing good, and you?

我過得還不錯啊，你呢？

例 I'm pretty good, thank you.

我也很好啊，謝謝。

會話 2

例 I have heard you're married!

我聽説你結婚了！

例 Yeah, I am. It happened so fast.

對啊，一切都發生的好快哦。

例 You are doing good!

你過得很好嘛！

🎧 track 009

一般般囉

Nothing special.

解析

感覺好像每次寒喧都要回答很好,但其實
也不一定,有時候真的生活沒有什麼特別
的事情發生,自己也沒有特別覺得很好,
就可以說一般般囉。

會話 1

例 How was your weekend?

你週末過得怎樣?

例 Nothing special.

一般般囉。

會話 2

例 How was your date?

約會還好嗎?

例 It was fine. Nothing special.

還好啦,沒什麼特別的。

沒有什麼特別的

As usual.

解析

意思就是和平常沒什麼差別,用於回答沒有什麼特別的情況。

會話

例 Did you have a crazy birthday party this time?

你這次的生日派對有什麼特別的嗎?

例 As usual. Cakes and balloons.

沒有什麼特別的,一樣蛋糕和汽球。

會話

例 What are you going to do this weekend?

你這個週末要幹嘛?

例 I am going hiking with my family as usual.

一如往常的和我家人去健行。

🎧track 010

我不想提起(不太好)
I don't want to talk about it.

解析

常別人問起而自己對於情況不太滿意的時候,可以用這句話來停止有關的話題。

會話1

例 How was your interview?
面試還好嗎?

例 I don't want to talk about it.
別提了。

會話2

例 I have heard about your mother.
Do you want to talk about it?
我聽說你媽媽的事了,你需要聊聊嗎?

例 No thanks, I don't want to talk about it now.
謝謝,沒關係,現在不太想講這件事。

不好意思

Excuse me

解析

第一：可用在借過或是禮貌性的說不好意思。

第二：有對不起的意思。

會話 1

例 Excuse me, can you pass me the salt?
不好意思，可以請你把鹽遞給我嗎？

例 Here you are.
給你。

會話 2

例 Excuse me, do you know where the gas station is?
對不起，請問你知道加油站在哪嗎？

例 I'm sorry, I don't know.
不好意思，我不知道。

track 011

我的榮幸
My pleasure!

解 析

等同於 You are welcome. 不客氣的意思，也可以用 My pleasure 替代。另一種解釋可以當作感到榮幸。

會 話 1

例 Thank you for your help.
謝謝你的幫忙。

例 It's my pleasure.
哪裡，是我的榮幸。

會 話 2

例 Can I have the pleasure to be your guide?
我有這個榮幸成為你們的嚮導嗎？

例 You are too kind.
你人真是太好了。

我想是吧

I guess.

解析

「我想是吧」、「大概吧」。也可以說I guess so. 或是I think so. 帶有不太確定的肯定語氣。

會話 1

例 Do you think the weather is going to be nice tomorrow?

你覺得明天會是好天氣嗎？

例 I think so.

我想會吧。

會話 2

例 I have heard that your girlfriend is super rich!

我聽說你女朋友超級有錢的！

例 I guess.

大概吧。

track 012

喔，原來如此

I see.

解 析

非常簡單的 I see. 其實在對話中可以化解許多尷尬及遇到不知如何回話的場面。代表著「喔，原來如此」、「嗯嗯」或是「我知道了」。

會話 1

例 My parents got divorced, so I am living with my dad now.

我父母離婚了，所以我現在跟爸爸住。

例 I see. I'm sorry.

我了解了，我感到很遺憾。

會話 2

例 Maybe it is time for our relationship to take a short break.

也許我們現在應該暫時分開冷靜一下。

例 Ok, I see. Are you breaking up with me?

我知道了。你現在是要跟我分手嗎？

待會見!

See ya!

解 析

有時候説再見不會直接説bye而是用待會兒見來表示,原本是 See you. 但是因為講的很快就會變成See ya囉。

會 話 1

例 I have to go, see you tomorrow.
我該走了,明天見囉。

例 See ya.
再見。

會 話 2

例 I am off to work, hope to see you again.
我要去上班了,希望下次再看到你。

例 Ok, see ya.
好的,下次見。

Chapter

2

家人

我想跟你們聊聊
I need to speak with you.

解析

家人之間總是會討論到許多問題，這時就可以使用這句話，如果需要更有禮貌一點，可以加 May 變成 May I speak with you?

會話 1

例 Mom, may I speak with you? It is about my English class.

媽，我想跟你聊一下有關於我的英文課。

例 Sure, what happened?

當然可以，怎麼了嗎？

會話 2

例 I need to speak with you, right now!

我現在必須跟你們聊聊。

例 Dad, we did not break the vase, it was the dog.

爸，不是我們打破花瓶，是狗狗打破的。

你們根本不了解我！
You don't know me!

解 析

這句話常常出現在青年少正值青春期，總是會希望父母親更為諒解、希望自己的行為能被接受，所以當受到拒絕或是阻礙的時候，就會覺得父母根本不了解自己。

會 話 1

例 Why is being a circus clown not a profession?

為什麼當馬戲團小丑就不是正常職業？

例 We want you to have stable income.

我們只是希望你能有穩定的工作。

例 You don't know me! This is what I really want to do!

你們根本不了解我，這才是我想要的！

這都是為了你好。

It is for your own good.

解析

這句話也有另一個說法是This is for your own sake. 一樣是「都是為了你好」的意思。也是常常父母親會掛在嘴邊的話。

會話1

例 You should eat breakfast every day, and do you know why?
你應該每天都要吃早餐，你知道為什麼嗎？

例 I know. It is for my own good.
我知道，是為了我好嘛。

會話2

例 They seem to be not very good friends.
他們感覺是些三教九流的朋友。

例 So you don't want me to see them anymore?
所以是叫我不要跟他們來往嗎？

例 It's for your own sake.
這是為了你好。

我想我可以處理
I think I can handle it.

解析

當對方質疑自己的能力是否足以面對問題時，如果對自己有信心，就可以說I think I can handle it. 表示自己可以處理這件事。

會話 1

例 If someone is bullying you, you should let us know!
如果有人欺負你，你一定要跟我們說！

例 Thanks, dad, but I think I can handle it.
謝啦老爸，不過我想我可以自己處理好這件事。

會話 2

例 All you need to do is cover for me in front of Mom and Dad.
你只需要在爸媽面前幫我掩護一下就好。

例 I don't think I can handle it.
　我想我沒辦法。

例 Please! You're my sister!
　拜託！你是我姐姐耶！

🎧 track 015

你真的很幼稚！

That's really immature!

解析

在人與人之間很常出現的對話，受不了對方幼稚的行為，在家人之間也常常用到。如果是嘲諷的口氣可以說 That's really mature.「真是太成熟了」或是 grow up!「可不可以長大一點！」

會話 1

例 You didn't want to listen to me so I don't want to listen to you.
　你剛剛沒聽我說話所以我現在也不想聽你說話。

例 That's really immature.
　真幼稚。

會 話 2

例 You are 30 years old and you don't have a job. You need to grow up!
你都三十歲了還不工作，你可以成熟一點嗎？

例 It is none of your business.
不用你管。

功課做完了嗎？

Have you finished your homework?

解 析

爸爸媽媽或是長輩最常問小孩的就是，你功課做完了沒？寫完功課才可以做別的事，所以會常常用到這句話。

會 話 1

例 Have you finished your homework?
功課都寫完了嗎？

例 Yes. All done!
全都寫完了！

會話 2

例 You know that you cannot play video games before you finish your homework.

你很清楚沒寫完功課不准玩電動。

例 But I have finished half of it!

可是我寫了一半了啦！

🎧 track 016

今天學校還好嗎？

How was school?

解析

在孩子放學回家後，通常父母親會問今天教了什麼，學校還好嗎之類的話，可以和孩子聊聊學校發生的事。School也可以改成class, work等等。

會話 1

例 Mom, I'm home.

媽我回來了。

例 Hey, how was school?

嗨，今天學校還好嗎？

會話 2

例 How was your dancing class?

舞蹈課上的如何？

例 It was really fun!

真的很好玩！

今天過得如何？

How was your day?

解析

在一天結束回到家時，通常這時候就可以問家人今天過得還好嗎？

會話 1

例 I'm home.

我到家了。

例 Hey, how was your day?

嘿今天還好嗎？

例 Pretty good.

還不錯啊。

會話 2

例 How was your first day at school?

第一天上學還好嗎？

例 Not bad, my classmates are pretty cool.

不錯啊，我同學都還滿酷的。

track 017

②
家
人

真是令人頭痛的一天！

What a day!

解 析

通常是有驚嘆的意思，除了表達很難熬的
一天，也可以用於這一天過的得令人感到
不可思議！

會話 1

例 What a day!

真是令人頭痛的一天！

例 Did your students give you a hard time
again?

你的學生又不聽話了嗎？

會話 2

例 I ran into my ex-girl friend when I was having dinner with my current girlfriend today.

我今天和我現在女朋友在吃飯的時候遇到我前女友。

例 What a day!

天啊！

感覺你今天不太順利？

Tough day at school / the office?

解 析

如果可以從一個人的臉上看出今天好像不太順利的表情，就可以直接問今天在辦公室/學校是不是遇到了什麼不開心的事。或是有時候是因為太忙也可以說 It was a long day.

會話 1

例 Tough day at school sweetie?

親愛的，今天學校不順利嗎？

例 Well, I think my history teacher does not like me.

我想我歷史老師真的很不喜歡我耶。

會話 2

例 Tough day at the office? You look so tired.

今天辦公室很忙嗎？你看起來好累。

例 It was a long day for sure.

今天真的還滿忙的。

🎧 track 018

你麻煩大了！
You are in big trouble!

解析

當某人闖了禍，比如說打破了花瓶，朋友來家裡玩把家裡搞得一團亂，旁邊的人就會跟他說：你麻煩大了！You are in a big trouble.

會話 1

例 I broke mom's vase.

我把媽媽的花瓶打破了。

例 You are in big trouble!

你麻煩大了！

會話 2

例 Did you just hang up the phone?

你剛剛是把電話掛掉嗎？

例 I thought there was no one there.

我以為電話那頭沒有人啊。

例 You are in big trouble. That was dad's boss on hold.

你完蛋了，那是爸爸的老闆在線上。

管好你自己！
Get yourself in line!

解析

當有人不守本分、逾矩，或是管太多閒事時，就可以告訴對方請先管好你自己就好。

會話 1

例 I don't think he is worthy for that reward.

我不認為他有資格可以拿到獎賞。

例 Get yourself in line before you talk about others.

先把你自己管好再去管別人好嗎。

會話2

例 Can you get your girlfriend in line? She is always nagging about my outfit!

可以管管你女朋友嗎？她每次都對我的穿著有意見！

例 I think she just cares about you, sis.

老妹，我想她只是表示關心。

例 Right.

最好是啦。

🎧 track 019

我以你為榮

I am proud of you.

解析

當對方做出一些值得鼓勵或是了不起的事，就可以大方分享自己有多麼以他為榮，為他感到開心。

會話 1

例 I got first place in the speech contest!
我演講比賽得了第一名！

例 I am so proud of you!
我真是太以你為榮了！

會話 2

例 It is not easy to make that decision,
I am very proud of you.
要做出這樣的決定不容易，你令我感到驕傲。

例 I am proud of myself, too.
我也為自己感到驕傲。

先說清楚

For the record….

解析

有鄭重申明的意思，特此強調的用法，日常生活中在即將講述一件事情之前，為了強調，可以説：「先説清楚哦，…」或是有「順便一提」的意思。

會話 1

例 Just for the record, smoking is not good for your health.

只是想強調一下,抽煙對你身體不好

例 I know, thank you.

我曉得,謝謝你。

會話 2

例 Just for the record, this is not a date, right?

只是想先説清楚,這不算是約會吧?

例 Of course not.

當然不是。

小·叮·嚀

也可以用 Just in case,有相似的意思: 順帶一提。

🎧 track 020

你應該修一下頭髮了

You need to trim your hair.

迷你短句

解析

當見到很熟的親朋好友頭髮太長很凌亂的話，可以提醒他時間到了該修剪一下頭髮了。

會話 1

例 You really need to trim your hair.
你真的應該要去剪一下頭髮。

例 I think it looks fine.
我覺得看起來還好啊。

會話 2

例 Do you have any plans tomorrow?
你明天有要做什麼嗎？

例 I need to trim my hair.
我需要去修一下頭髮。

不要再講有的沒有的了

**No more trash talk.
(Enough trash talk.)**

解 析

當聽到週遭的朋友和兄弟姐妹，或是小孩一直在講一些無關緊要的話，聽到很受不了的時候除了叫他們閉嘴 (shut up) 也可以用這句來表示。

會話 **1**

例 I bet the dog will eat its own poop.
我賭那隻狗會吃他自己的便便。

例 Haha, I'm in. What is your bet?
哈哈我跟了，你賭什麼？

例 Kids, no more trash talk, ok?
孩子們，不要再講這些有的沒有的了好嗎？

會話 **2**

例 Enough trash talk! Be serious!
不要講廢話了，認真一點好嗎！

例 Yes, ma'am.
是的女士！

2 家人

🎧 track 021

幾乎
Nearly / Almost

解析

這兩個字的意思都是：差不多，幾乎的意思。在日常生活中很常出現也很實用。

會話 1

例 I almost did not wake up on time.
我差點就睡過頭了。

例 Fortunately, I called you.
幸好我有打給你。

會話 2

例 Have you finished the paper?
你報告寫完了嗎？

例 Nearly.
差不多了。

你在瞞我什麼？

What are you not telling me?

解 析

如果感覺對方好像有事情在瞞著自己沒有說清楚時，可以很明白地問對方，你是不是有什麼事沒有告訴我。

會話 1

例 What are you not telling me?
你是不是有什麼事沒有跟我說呢？

例 I am pregnant.
我懷孕了。

會話 2

例 It is just a cold.
只是個小感冒而已。

例 It looks more than that. What are you not telling me?
看起來不止是感冒啊，你在瞞我什麼？

例 I just don't want you to worry.
我只是不想你擔心。

track 022

不要再嘮叨了

Stop nagging.

解 析

當有人一直在旁邊嘮嘮叨叨或是抱怨的時候，就可以用這句話請對方不要再嘮叨了。

會 話 1

例 I really don't like this party. Can you believe they serve this….

這個派對好爛哦，你相信嗎，他們提供這種……

例 Stop nagging. If you don't like it, you are free to go!

不要一直嘮叨啦，你不喜歡可以走啊！

會 話 2

例 You know what I always tell you: Don't scatter your clothes on the floor!

我是怎麼跟你說的: 不要把衣服亂丟在地上！

例 I know I know I know! Stop nagging!

我知道我知道我知道啦，不要再嘮叨了啦！

我完全了解

I completely understand.

解析

就好像是I know. 或是I see. 這裡會有一點強調我真的完全明白的意思，如果把completely 去掉也可以，或是用totally來代替。

會話1

例 It is not easy to raise three children you know?

要扶養三個小孩不是件容易的事你知道嗎？

例 I completely understand.

我完全了解。

會話2

例 This is too much for me.

我真的受夠了。

馬上說 生活英文
迷你短句

例 I totally understand.
我了解。

track 023

我感覺好多了
I am feeling much better now.

解析

不管是在情緒或是身體方面,當有人問起,你有比較好一點了嗎?除了回答I'm fine. 也可以說我現在感覺好多了。

例 Are you feeling any better?
你有好一點嗎?

例 Thank you. I am feeling much better now.
謝謝你,我好多了。

會話 2

例 I have a severe headache.
我現在頭超痛的。

068

例 Hope you will be feeling better soon.
希望你趕快好起來。

你還好嗎？
How are you holding up?

解析

通常是問對方，在這一連串的事件後，還撐得住嗎？還好嗎？有可能是經歷了一些較令人感到麻煩的事。

會話1

例 I heard your father is still in the hospital. How are you holding up?
我聽說你爸還在住院，你還好嗎？

例 I am doing fine, but I'm so tired.
我還好，只是很累。

會話2

例 Still preparing for your exam?
還在準備考試嗎？

例 Yup.

　　沒錯。

例 How are you holding up?

　　一切都還好嗎?

 ○track 024

我同意

I agree.

解析

若是認同對方的意見、說法,這時候就會
點點頭說:嗯嗯,我同意。

會話1

例 That was the best game ever!

　　那真的是有史以來最好看的比賽了!

例 I agree.

　　我同意。

會話2

例 Your father and I both agree that you
　　should go to college.

　　你爸跟我都同意你應該去唸大學。

例 I thought you want me to work.

我以為你們要我去工作。

他/她會很開心的

S / he will be delighted.

解析

Happy 也可以用 delighted 來表示,也是感到開心的、高興的。

會話 1

例 Tomorrow is Mom's birthday. We should give her a surprise.

明天是媽媽的生日,我們應該給她一個驚喜。

例 Yeah, she will be delighted.

好啊,她會很開心的。

會話 2

例 Oh,no. I forgot to buy dad's beer.

喔不,我忘記買爸爸的啤酒了。

例 He is not going to be delighted.

他可能不會太開心哦。

track 025

停止！
Knock it off!

解析

若是有人發生衝突或是打鬧的情況，這時候要喝止他們停止，就是說：Knock it off! 有「不要再玩了！不要再吵了！」的意思。

會話

例 Don't touch my robot.

不要碰我的機器人。

例 That's mine.

那是我的。

例 I don't see your name on it.

上面又沒有你的名字。

例 I said it's mine!

我說那是我的！

例 Hey! You two! Knock it off!

嘿你們兩個，不要吵了！

遲早的
Sooner or later.

解析

「這都是遲早的事啦」該怎麼說呢？只要加一個 sooner or later 整句話就會變得非常活靈活現了。

會話 1

例 You should tell your brother not to hang out with those friends.

你應該要跟你弟弟說不要跟那些朋友來往。

例 He will get his lesson sooner or later.

他遲早會學到教訓的

會話 2

例 If you keep acting like this, sooner or later he will leave you.

如果你繼續這樣下去，他遲早會離開你。

例 I know. That's why I'm doing this.

我知道，所以我才要這麼做

Chapter

3

朋友

隨時奉陪

Anytime!

解析

也是「任何時候」的時候，隨時、總是，
都可以使用到。

會話 1

例 What time is better for me to call?

我什麼時間打你比較方便？

例 Anytime!

隨時都可以。

會話 2

例 Thank you for your company.

謝謝你陪我。

例 Anytime!

沒有問題！

真是受不了他／她！

I can't put up with him/her anymore!

解析

有時候當很受不了某人的言行，就會不免跟朋友抱怨一下，這句話就很好用，表示真的是受夠了。

會話1

例 I can't put up with her anymore!
我真受不了她了！

例 What did she do this time?
她這次又做了什麼好事？

會話2

例 What's wrong? You look upset.
怎麼了，你看起來很生氣

例 I just can't put up with my boyfriend anymore.
我再也不能忍受我男朋友了

可不是嗎！

Tell me about it!

解析

當認同對方所說的話時，可以接著說這句表示再同意不過了。

會話1

例 Oh my god, the weather is crazy hot!
我的天啊，天氣也太熱了吧！

例 Tell me about it!
可不是嗎！

會話2

例 I do not understand why people want to get married.
我不懂為什麼有人會想結婚。

例 Tell me about it.
就是說啊。

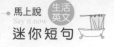

小·叮·嚀

字面上很像，但是這裡不是指：跟我說說發生什麼事了哦！

我有一個瘋狂的點子！

I've got an idea!

解析

通常這句話可以用在，突然想到什麼好主意可以解決眼前的問題時。

會話 1

例 I am in a relationship crisis….

我陷入了感情危機……

例 I've got an idea!

我有一個好主意！

會話 2

例 I've got an idea!

我想到一個瘋狂的點子！

例 Which is?

是什麼？

例 Let's get married now!

我們現在就去結婚！

 track 028

不可能！

Impossible!

解析

有「少來！不可能！不可置信！」的意思。

會話1

例 I won the lottery.

我中樂透了。

例 Impossible.

少來。

會話2

例 I like you more than you like me.

我喜歡你比你喜歡我還多。

例 Impossible.

不可能。

門都沒有！

No way! / Not a chance.

解析

很實用的生活日常對話，常常會聽到有人用 No way! 或是 Not a chance! 表示休想，門都沒有！

會話 1

例 Can I borrow NT$10,000 from you?

我可以跟你借一萬塊嗎？

例 No way!

門都沒有！

會話 2

例 I was wondering maybe we could….

我在想也許我們倆個可以……

例 Not a chance.

休想，不可能。

track 029

那個帥哥真可愛

He is really cute.

解析

跟好朋友在一起時總免不了會八卦一下，如果欣賞某個男生，就可以跟朋友分享。

會話 1

例 Do you know that guy? He is really cute.

你認識那個男生嗎，他真的好帥哦。

例 Yeah, he is my cousin.

知道啊，他是我表哥。

會話 2

例 Is that guy over there your boyfriend?

那邊那個是你男朋友嗎？

例 Ex boyfriend.

前男友。

例 I don't know why you broke up, but he is super cute.

我不知道你們為什麼分手，但是他真的非常可愛。

那個女的好正

She (That chick) is hot.

解析

如果用在女生身上，就可以說那個女生好正、好辣。

會話 1

例 That girl is hot.

那個女孩好辣。

例 You should go talk to her.

你應該去跟她說說話。

會話 2

例 That chick is super hot.

那個女生超級正。

例 Really? She is my sister.

真的嗎？她是我妹。

🎧 track 030

不錯哦

Sweet! / Nice / Lovely
(It is really neat!)

解析

短短的幾個字也可以讓你表示驚呼,好記又達意!這些字可以在冷場或是不知道要接什麼話的時候用到。

會話 1

例 My family lives in a small town near the city. It's really beautiful.

我家人住在城市附近的小鎮上,那裡很美。

例 Nice!

哇,不錯啊!

會話 2

例 I got you a tuna sandwich.

我幫你買了一個鮪魚三明治。

例 Sweet!

太棒了！

我快沒時間了

I am running out of time!

解析

生活實用句子，很急忙的情況下，就可以說「我沒時間了啦！」

會話1

例 Can you please hurry up? I am running out of time.

你可以快一點嗎，我快沒時間了。

例 One minute!

再一分鐘！

會話2

例 I don't know what to wear tonight.

我不知道今天晚上到底要穿什麼。

例 We are running out of time. The reservation is at 8.

我們快沒有時間了，我訂八點的位子。

別傻了！

Don't be silly!

解 析

某一個情況是，在對話中，聽到不可思議的事，或是不相信對方的說法，可以使用；另一種是，希望對方不要胡思亂想。

會 話 1

例 Do you think Mark will marry me?

你覺得馬克會娶我嗎？

例 Don't be silly!

別傻了！

會 話 2

例 I don't think you like me anymore.

我覺得你好像不喜歡我了。

例 Don't be silly! Of course I do.

別傻了，我當然喜歡。

③
朋
友

隨機應變吧！

Improvising!

解析

在遇到不知道接下來該怎麼辦的時候，就得隨機應變，這時就可以用到，非常實用。

會話 1

例 What's next?

那現在該怎麼辦？

例 Improvising!

隨機應變吧！

會話 2

例 What is your suggestion?

所以你的建議是？

例 I don't know. Improvising?

我不曉得，隨機應變吧？

沒問題
No problem.

解析

一種情況是，回答對方的請求；另一種情況可以用在，當對方答謝時，表示只是小事一樁不足掛齒。

會話 1

例 Can you pick me up at 7?

你可以七點來接我嗎？

例 No problem.

沒問題。

會話 2

例 Thank you very much.

真是非常感謝你。

例 No problem.

沒什麼。

我玩得很開心

I really enjoyed myself.

解析

和朋友過了美好的時光，可以用到這句話表示自己玩得很開心。

會話 1

例 How was your day with your friends?
你今天和朋友出去好玩嗎？

例 Nice. I really enjoyed myself.
我玩得很開心

會話 2

例 Enjoy yourself, and be careful!
玩得開心點，也要小心哦！

例 Thanks,
謝啦。

有新鮮事嗎？

Anything new?

解析

與朋友一見面時除了問你好嗎？How are
you doing? 也可以順便問最近有什麼特別
的事發生嗎？

會話 1

例 Hey, anything new?

嘿，最近有什麼新鮮事嗎？

例 My wife is pregnant.

我老婆懷孕了。

會話 2

例 Anything new?

最近有什麼特別的事嗎？

例 I got fired.

我被開除了。

③ 朋友

也太可笑了吧！

How droll!

解析

用於形容滑稽可笑的人或事，有點不同於 funny 的地方是，funny 是比較有趣好笑的意思，而 droll 有不屑、可笑的感覺。

會話1

例 Look at my new hair style!

看我的新髮型！

例 How droll!

也太滑稽了吧！

會話2

例 Did you see his droll expression?

你有看到他那好笑的表情嗎？

例 He looks like a clown.

他像個小丑。

隨時更新消息啊！

Keep me posted!

解析

非常頻繁使用的句子，類似Let me know.
除了有「記得讓我知道」，也有隨時有什
麼消息，要趕快通知我。

會話 1

例 I am not so sure right now.

我現在還不是很確定。

例 Ok, then. Keep me posted.

好吧，那再隨時讓我知道最新消息。

會話 2

例 Next time we meet will be in one year.

下次見面就是一年後了。

例 Keep me posted, ok?

隨時讓我知道你的近況好嗎？

例 Of course, take care.

當然，保重了。

3 朋友

讓我確認一下

Let me check.

解析

除了有「讓我確認,再回覆你」的用法之外,也可以照字面上的意思,讓我看一下、讓我檢查一下 Let me see.

會話1

例 Are you free tomorrow afternoon? Sandy wants to meet us and have a cup of coffee.

你明天下午有空嗎?珊迪想要見面喝杯咖啡。

例 Let me check.

讓我確認一下。

會話2

例 I just cut myself. Do you have a bandage?

我剛剛割到自己了,你有繃帶嗎?

例 Let me check.

我看一下哦。

🎧 track 035

一定會很好玩的！
It will be fun!

解析

用來表示興奮之情，可能要出去玩了，或者是要說服朋友一起參加，就可以用這句 "It will be fun!"

會話 1

例 Do you want to join us? It will be fun!
你要來嗎？一定會很好玩的！

例 I don't know. I don't feel so well today.
我不知道耶，我今天不太舒服。

會話 2

例 Can I bring my friends too?
我也可以帶我朋友一起嗎？

例 Of course! It will be fun!
當然可以，一定會很好玩的！

3 朋友

相信你的直覺

What's your gut telling you?

解析

Gut 的意思是腸子，但也有勇氣、膽量、直覺的意思，這裡是指相信自己的直覺。

會話1

例 I don't know what to do.

我不知道該怎麼辦。

例 What is your gut telling you?

你的直覺告訴你該怎麼做？

會話2

例 My gut is telling me to leave.

我的直覺告訴我要離開這裡。

例 So there!

那就這樣啊！

放輕鬆點

Take it easy.

解析

告訴對方,這件事沒有什麼,不要那麼緊張也不要那麼拘謹的時候,除了説Relax,也可以使用這句Take it easy.

會話 1

例 I am going to see his parents tomorrow. What if they don't like me?

我明天就要去見他爸媽了,萬一他們不喜歡我怎麼辦?

例 Take it easy. It will be fine.

放輕鬆,一切都會很好的。

會話 2

例 You need to take it easy.

你需要放輕鬆一點。

例 You are not the one who is going to see the dentist.

又不是你要去看牙醫。

③ 朋友

萬歲！太好了！

Hooray!

解析

感嘆語氣：好耶！太好了！好極了！萬歲！在很開心很興奮的時候使用。

會話1

例 I won the first prize!

我贏得頭獎耶！

例 Hooray!

太棒了！

會話2

例 We are going to Brazil this summer!

我們這個暑假要去巴西玩！

例 Hooray!

好耶！

不要放我鴿子

Don't stand me up!

解 析

與朋友有約，最常出現的突發狀況就是遲到或是被放鴿子，這時候就可以先警告對方，不要放我鴿子！

會話 1

例 I will see you tomorrow morning.
明天早上見。

例 Don't stand me up again.
不要再放我鴿子囉。

會話 2

例 Don't stand me up this time. It is a very important dinner.

不要放我鴿子，這次的晚餐真的很重要。

例 I promise.
我保證不會。

3 朋友

他/她放我鴿子！

S / he stood me up!

解 析

在之前提過的放鴿子是還沒有發生的，這時候已經發生了，就會變成生氣的語氣了！

會 話 1

例 How could you stand me up?

你怎麼可以放我鴿子？

例 I'm so sorry. I really forgot.

對不起，我是真的忘記了。

會 話 2

例 How was your date?

你的約會如何？

例 She stood me up.

她放我鴿子。

🎧 track 038

我們講的是同一件事嗎？

Are we on the same page?

解析

其實這句話有一些不同的用法，除了「我們講的是同一件事嗎？」還有「我們有達成共識嗎？」等等的說法，在你不確定對方是不是在跟你講同一件事的時候，你就可以這樣說。

會話1

例 Are we on the same page? I am talking about my sister's wedding.

我們在講同一件事嗎？我說的是我妹妹的婚禮耶。

例 Oh, I thought you are talking about Sally.

喔，我還以為你在講莎莉呢。

會話 2

例 I totally agree with you. It was a big mistake.

我完全同意你的説法，這件事真是錯的離譜。

例 Uhhh, I don't think we are on the same page.

嗯…我想我們講的是不同一件事。

面對現實吧！
Deal with it!

解析

也可以用 Face it! 意指遇到困難或是不順心的事，還是得咬著牙接受它，接受擺在眼前的事實。

會話 1

例 She will not go out with you, just deal with it!

她是不會跟你約會的，面對現實吧！

例 But I really like her.
但我真的很喜歡她啊。

會話 **2**

例 I still cannot believe this.
我還是不敢相信。

例 Deal with it, we are broke.
接受事實吧,我們破產了。

track 039

希望如此

I wish.

解析

遇到力不從心的事情,都會說:我也希望
能…。但是通常都是無法改變的事實。

會話 **1**

例 I promise I will visit you soon.
我保證我很快會去看你。

例 I wish.
希望是這樣。

會話 2

例 I could never lie to you.

我永遠都不可能對你說謊。

例 I wish.

希望如此。

你在開玩笑吧？

Are you kidding me?

解析

聽到自己不敢置信的事情就可以用這句
話，「你是認真的嗎？」「你在開我玩笑
吧？」

會話 1

例 This bag cost me NT$10,000.

這個包包花了我一萬塊。

例 Are you kidding me?

你跟我開玩笑吧？

會話 2

例 I won NT\$20,000,000 in the lottery.
我贏了樂透二千萬元。

例 Are you kidding me?
你真認真的嗎？

∩ track 040

沒關係

Don't bother.

解析

就是「沒關係」「不用麻煩了」的意思。

會話 1

例 Do you need something to drink?
你需要喝點什麼嗎？

例 Don't bother. I'm fine.
不用麻煩了。

會話 2

例 Don't you think we should tell him the truth?
你不覺得我們應該要告訴他真相嗎？

例 Don't bother, he will figure it out sooner or later.

沒關係啦，他遲早會知道的。

好奇怪哦

That is weird.

解 析

遇到覺得很奇怪，或是很想不透的事情，就可以說：真的好奇怪哦。也可以用在人身上，譬如 S/he is weird. 她/他好奇怪哦。

會 話1

例 Did you see my wallet? I put it here.

你有看到我的皮包嗎？我放在這裡啊。

例 Nope.

沒有耶。

例 That is weird.

奇怪了。

會 話 2

例 She has not eaten for the whole day; that is so weird.

她一整天都沒吃飯，好奇怪哦。

例 Maybe she is sick.

也許她生病了。

 ∩track 041

你隨時都可以來訪

You can drop by anytime.

解 析

當跟朋友說再見時，也歡迎下次再來玩，就可以對朋友說：隨時來拜訪啊！或者另一個也有歡迎隨時參觀的意思。

會 話 1

例 See you next time.

下次見囉。

例 Drop by anytime!

隨時來拜訪唷！

會話 2

例 You can drop by anytime to see our new product.

你可以隨時來參觀我們的新產品。

例 Ok, no problem.

好的，沒問題。

你死定了！

You are going down!

解析

這句話也是和 You are in big trouble. 同意思，表示：「你死定了！你完蛋了！」，通常就是在對方做了誇張不可原諒的事情時，就可以這樣說。

會話 1

例 Did you just tell my boyfriend that I went out with his friend?

你是不是跟我男朋友說我跟他朋友出去玩？

例 I think so....

好像是……

例 You are going down!

你死定了！

會話 2

例 Your mother just called.

你媽媽剛剛有打來。

例 Damn, I'm going down.

完了，我死定了。

 🎧 track 042

撐著點

Hang on.

解 析

為別人加油打氣時，就可以使用這句話，
希望朋友繼續堅持下去，不要放棄，也可
以說 Hang in there. 另外也有電話中不要
掛斷的意思。

會話 1

例 I don't know what to do.

我不知道該怎麼辦。

例 Hang in there. Everything will be fine.

撐著點,會否極泰來的。

會話 2

例 I don't think they can hang on much longer.

我覺得他們撐不了多久的了。

例 What makes you think so?

為什麼你會這麼認為?

他抓狂了

He snapped.

解析

形容一個人突然間抓狂、失去理智,就像理智線突然被折斷一樣。

會話 1

例 We should not have told him the news.

我們不應該跟他講這個消息的。

例 What happened?

發生什麼事了？

例 He just snapped.

他整個抓狂。

會 話 2

例 When he heard that he has to pay for
the car accident, he snapped.

當他聽到他必須為了這次車禍賠償，他就
抓狂了。

例 Of course! It was not his fault at all!

當然會！那又不是他的錯！

 track 043

算了吧！

Drop it!

解 析

字面上來說是放下，也就是希望對方可以
不要再計較了，通常我們就會說：哎唷，
算了吧。

會話 1

例 Why did she dump me?

她為什麼要跟我分手？

例 Drop it! You deserve better!

算了吧！你值得更好的！

會話 2

例 I want to win the lottery.

我想要贏樂透。

例 Drop it! Maybe you need to get a job first.

算了吧！也許你應該先找個工作。

相信我

Believe me, I know.

解析

告訴對方自己真的很了解這件事情、這個人或是這個情況的時候，就可以說：相信我，我比誰都清楚。

會話 1

例 How can you be so sure that he is not a good guy?

你怎麼能這麼確定他不是一個好人？

例 Girl, I'm 40. Believe me, I know.

孩子，我40歲了，相信我，我知道的。

會話 2

例 I don't think you know the consequence of this matter.

我不認為你知道事情的嚴重性。

例 Believe me, I know.

我比誰都了解。

 track 044

不敢相信！

Unbelievable!

解析

驚嘆的語氣，就是難以置信的意思。超乎自己可以想像的地步。

會話 1

例 Wow, you made this cake?

哇，這蛋糕是你做的嗎？

例 Yes, I did.

沒錯。

例 This is unbelievable!

簡直不敢相信！

會話 2

例 Did you know she is dating a 48-year-old guy?

你知道她跟一個48歲的老男人交往嗎？

例 Unbelievable.

我不敢相信。

認真的嗎？

Seriously?

解析

其實這句話非常的好用，有時候意思很像 Are you kidding me? 就是有「你在跟我開玩笑嗎？」的意思，另外也有不可置信的意思。

會話 1

例 Your dorm is on fire.

你的宿舍著火了。

例 Seriously?

認真的嗎？

例 Nope, haha.

不是啊，哈哈。

會話 2

例 You bought a NT$50,000 bike, seriously?

你真的花了五萬元買一台腳踏車嗎？

例 It is not just a bike!

那不是一輛普通的腳踏車！

🎧 track 045

還差的遠呢！

Not even close.

解析

除了是字面上距離的表達，另外在某些情況上也是告訴對方說：你還差的遠呢！或是非常不可能的意思。

會話 1

例 Is this the right answer?

這個答案是正確的嗎？

例 Not even close.

還差的遠呢。

會話 2

例 Do you think that team can win the game?

你覺得那隊會贏嗎？

例 Not even close.

想太多了。

講重點

Cut to the chase.

解析

這句話的意思就是，希望對方可以省略前面一堆有的沒有的話，直接切入重點。

會話 1

例 I want to make it clear that after all these things…

經過這麼多事情後我想說的是……

例 Just cut to the chase, please.

拜託講重點就好。

會話 2

例 Don't you think it is weird that she came back so late?

你不覺得她這麼晚回來很奇怪嗎？

例 No.

不會啊。

例 But didn't you see her makeup?

但你有看到她的妝嗎？

例 Can you just cut to the chase?

你到底想說什麼？

track 046

還不是很確定

It is still up in the air.

解析

如果在談論什麼計畫或是決定，當還沒有結論，或是還在討論當中的時候，就可以說這件事 still up in the air.

會話 1

例 So you will move to Australia when you get married?

所以你們結婚後會搬去澳洲？

例 It is still up in the air.

我們還沒決定。

會話 2

例 What is the plan for Teddy's birthday party?

泰迪的生日派對計畫是什麼？

例 I don't know. It is still up in the air.

不知道，還在討論。

我不介意
None taken.

解析

有「沒關係」的意思，與 never mind 類似，通常對方會在不當的行為或是言語之後自覺然後道歉，這時候如果不在意的話表示原諒就會說：None taken.

會話 1

例 Not everyone has your sexy big butt. No offense, I don't mean your butt is big.

不是每個人都有你的性感大屁股。抱歉，我不是指你屁股大。

例 None taken.

我不介意啦。

會話 2

例 I'm really sorry that I forgot to invite you.

我真的感到非常抱歉我忘記邀請你了。

3 朋友

迷你短句

例 It's ok. None taken.

沒關係啦，我不介意。

🎧 track 047

試試看啊

Try me.

解析

人家都說，沒試過說怎麼會知道呢？所以這個時候就可以說：試試看啊！

會話 **1**

例 Forget it. You will not believe what I am going to tell you.

算了，你不會相信我要說什麼的。

例 Try me.

告訴我試試看啊。

會話 **2**

例 You don't have the guts to take the challenge.

你才沒有膽量接受挑戰。

例 Really? Try me.

真的嗎？試看看啊。

我不記得了

Not that I recall.

解析

就像 I don't remember. 我不記得了。意思
是一樣的，只是也可以這麼說來表示自己
不記得有這件事。

3
朋
友

會話 1

例 She had a car accident a few years
ago, right?

她幾年前出過一次車禍對不對？

例 Not that I recall.

我不記得了耶。

會話 2

例 Where did you park your car?

你把車停哪了啊？

迷你短句

例 I don't recall. I was too tired.

我不記得了，我實在太累了。

track 048

你在呼嚨我

You are bluffing.

解析

這句話通常是用在表示「虛張聲勢」。指某些人只是嘴巴上說說不會真的去做。

會話 1

例 Don't listen to him, he is just bluffing.

別聽他的，他只是在虛張聲勢。

例 But he looks so serious.

但是他看起來好認真。

會話 2

例 I will kick your ass!

我會教訓你一頓！

例 You are bluffing.

你只是在呼嚨我。

不然你想怎樣！

Bite me!

解析

其實它的意思就是：不然你能拿我怎樣！
有一種挑釁的感覺，不過是無傷大雅的玩
笑話。

會話 1

例 How could you eat my cookies without
telling me?

你怎麼可以沒有我說一聲就吃了我的餅
乾？

例 Bite me!

不然你想怎樣！

會話 2

例 That is not nice!

這樣很不好耶！

例 Or what? Bite me!

不然你能拿我怎樣？

track 049

只是個私人笑話

It's just a private joke.

解析

只有自己懂自己在笑什麼，或是只有自己跟特定的人才懂的笑話就是私人笑話，所以有時候會看到某些人自己笑得很開心，別人卻不知道他到底在笑什麼。

會話 1

例 Why are you laughing?

你在笑什麼？

例 Nothing, it's just a private joke.

沒什麼，只是個私人笑話。

會話 2

例 Why is he laughing?

他為什麼在笑？

例 Maybe he just remembered something funny. It's his private joke, I think.

也許他只是想到什麼有趣的事，他自己的笑話啦。

他/她有時候很愛指使人

S / he is so bossy sometimes.

解 析

Bossy有跋扈的、愛指使別人的意思，有些人很愛叫你去做這做那的，又一副理所當然的樣子，自以為是你的老闆，這時候就會說那個人很跋扈。

③ 朋友

會 話 1

例 Her boyfriend's mother is pretty bossy.
她男朋友的媽媽很跋扈。

例 That's why they broke up?
所以他們才分手嗎？

會 話 2

例 Don't be so bossy, I don't work for you.
不要這麼愛指使人，我又不是你的員工

例 Sorry, I can't help it.
抱歉，習慣很難改

Chapter

4

情人

track 050

我不喜歡你的態度

I don't like the way you behave.

解析

當情人在吵架的時候，一定是因為某件事而觸發了地雷，這時可能是因為其中一方的態度不是很好，而導致另一方說出這樣的話。

會話1

例 I don't like the way you behave.
我不喜歡你這樣的態度。

例 What? I said I am sorry.
什麼？我已經說對不起了啊？

會話2

例 Whatever.
隨便你啊。

例 I don't like the way you said that.
我不喜歡你口氣。

我們需要談談

We need to talk.

解析

這應該是情侶之間最不想聽到的一句話了，通常在講這句話的時候，表示有很嚴重的事情想要與對方討論。

會話 1

例 We need to talk.

我們需要談一談。

例 That is the last thing I want to hear.

這真是我最不想聽到的一句話了。

會話 2

例 Don't you think we need to talk about this?

你不認為我們應該好好談談嗎？

例 There is nothing to talk about.

根本沒有什麼好談的啊。

track 051

我道歉

My apologies.

解析

除了說 I am sorry. 之外，My apologies. 也是有我道歉、都是我的不對的意思，也有更慎重的意味。

會話 1

例 My apologies.

都是我不好。

例 It's too late.

太遲了。

會話 2

例 Is there anything you want to say?

你還有什麼想說的嗎？

例 I am sorry. My apologies.

我很抱歉，都是我的不對。

4
情
人

接受你的道歉

Apology accepted.

解析

好像大部份的人都會說對不起，可是卻很少聽到人家說：好吧，原諒你。所以這裡告訴大家的就是如何說「原諒你」。

會話 1

例 I am really sorry babe.
寶貝我真的很抱歉。

例 Ok···, apology accepted.
好啦，原諒你。

會話 2

例 Why didn't you say hi in the food court?
你剛剛在餐廳為什麼不跟我打招呼？

例 I did not see you, sorry!
我沒有看到你啊，對不起！

例 All right, apology accepted.
好吧，接受你的道歉。

原諒你

You are forgiven.

解 析

「原諒你」其實就和「道歉被接受」是大同小異的意思，有很多種說法可以使用。

會 話 1

例 I did not mean to say that.
　我不是故意要那樣說的。

例 It's ok. You are forgiven.
　沒關係，我已經原諒你了。

會 話 2

例 Will you forgive me?
　你會原諒我嗎？

例 Ok⋯, but there is no next time.
　好啦⋯但沒有下一次囉。

小·叮·嚀

Forgive 也可以當作主動，可以說 Please forgive me. 「請原諒我」或是 I forgive you. 「我原諒你」。

❹
情
人

你在生我的氣嗎？

Are you mad at me?

解析

情侶之間鬧脾氣總會有不知所措的時候，搞不清楚狀況的人就會問：你在生我的氣嗎？

會話 1

例 You look upset. Are you mad at me?
你看起來很不開心，你在生我的氣嗎？

例 What do you think?
你覺得呢？

會話 2

例 Don't talk to me.
不要跟我講話。

例 Why? Please don't be mad.
為什麼？拜託不要生氣啦。

請給我一個合理的解釋
Please explain.

解析

人與人吵架總是希望對方可以好好解釋以化解誤會,這時候就可以說:請解釋。表示你給對方一個解釋的機會。

會話1

例 It is not what you think it is.
事情不是你所想的那樣。

例 Really? Please explain.
真的嗎?那你解釋一下。

會話2

例 I can explain.
我可以解釋。

例 I don't want to know.
我並不想聽。

很抱歉，我剛剛太衝動了
I am sorry; I was impulsive.

解析

吵架時因為心直口快，講了一些很衝動的話，冷靜後，跟對方道歉的時候可以說一下剛剛是因為太衝動了才會講出那些傷人的話。

會話 1

例 I do not like what you said.
我不喜歡你剛說的那些話。

例 I am sorry; I was impulsive.
對不起，我剛剛太衝動了。

會話 2

例 You should not have said that to your parents.
你剛不應該對你父母說那些話的。

例 I know. I was too impulsive.
我知道，我太衝動了。

很想你
Thinking of you.

解析

就如同一般情侶常常會説的話：很愛你、很想你，之類的肉麻小情話，可是卻也很甜蜜。

會話1

例 How are you doing, sweetie?
親愛的，你好嗎？

例 I'm good. Thinking of you.
我很好啊，很想你。

會話2

例 I miss you so bad.
我超級想你。

例 I miss you, too.
我也很想你。

情人

晚安美夢

Sweet dreams.

解 析

除了晚安之外,也可以祝對方有個美夢唷。

會 話 1

例 Good night. Sweet dreams.
晚安美夢。

例 Thank you.
謝謝你。

會 話 2

例 Sweet dreams.
祝美夢。

例 You too.
你也是。

我來付
I got it.

解析

記得每次男朋友要付錢時都會說這句：I got it. (我來就好) 所以其實女生如果表示貼心要付錢的時候，也可以很man說：I got it.

會話 1

例 How much?
這樣是多少？

例 I got it.
我付就好。

會話 2

例 I got it.
我付就好。

例 No! It's my turn this time.
不行！這次換我了。

④ 情人

就順其自然吧

Just go with the flow.

解析

常常遇到不知該如何決擇的情況，這時就
會說：那就順其自然吧。英文也是可以這
麼說：Just go with the flow.

會話1

例 Well, what do we do now?
那麼我們現在該怎麼辦？

例 Just go with the flow.
就順其自然吧。

會話2

例 So are you going to go back to your
boyfriend?
所以你會回到你男友身邊嗎？

例 I don't know. Just go with the flow.
我也不知道，就順其自然吧。

永遠不要說永遠

Never say never.

解析

就是向對方表示,一切事情都很難說,不要太快下定論。

會話 1

例 I think my boyfriend never wants to get married.

我覺得我男朋友永遠不會想結婚。

例 Never say never.

永遠不要說永遠。

會話 2

例 I would never like children.

我永遠都不會喜歡小孩的。

例 Never say never. You can't be sure.

話別說的太早哦。

很難說
You never know.

解 析

同樣與never say never有異曲同工之處，
意指很多事情都很難講，話先不要說死。

會話 1

例 He seems to be a very nice guy. He
will be a good husband, too.
他看起來是個好男人，一定也會是個好老
公。

例 You never know.
很難說哦。

會話 2

例 I would never ever fall in love with
a fat guy.
我絕對絕對不會愛上胖子的。

例 You never know.
很難說哦。

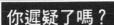

你遲疑了嗎？
Are you having second thoughts?

解 析

通常是指原本說好的事情有一方突然遲疑，其實是指比較不能被接受的。如果出現在情人間，就好像原本說好要結婚，有一方突然怯場。這時也會看到cold feet.

會 話 1

例 About moving in together, I think we need more discussion.

關於同居這件事，我覺得我們應該再討論一下。

例 Are you having second thoughts?

你現在是不想跟我住了嗎？

會 話 2

例 Do you think that David will get cold feet before the wedding?

你覺得大衛會在婚禮前臨陣脫逃嗎？

❹ 情人

例 Don't think about that.
千萬不要這樣想。

我為你感到開心
I am happy for you.

解析

當對方有什麼好消息時，這時候同理心也會給對方很大的支持與鼓勵。

會話1

例 Honey! I just became the new project manager!
親愛的，我剛剛升職為新的專案經理！

例 Really? I am so happy for you!
真的嗎？實在是太好了！

會話2

例 Thank god I am not pregnant.
好佳在我沒有懷孕。

例 I am happy for you.
我替你感到開心。

傷害已經造成了
The damage is done.

解 析

如果對方做了什麼不可原諒或是無法挽回的事，就會說：傷害都已經造成了，接下來還能怎麼辦呢？

會 話 1

例 The damage is done.
傷害已經造成了。

例 I can make it up to you.
我可以彌補你。

會 話 2

例 I feel so sorry.
我感到非常抱歉。

例 The damage is done. What can you do?
傷害已經造成了，還能怎麼辦呢？

你答應我的！
You gave me your word!

解析

若是對方食言或是不守信用的時候，就可以說：你答應過我的耶！提醒對方自己說過什麼話。也可以說：You promise! 有承諾的意思。

會話1

例 I am afraid that we cannot go to Europe this summer.

恐怕我們這個暑假無法去歐洲玩了。

例 Why? You gave me your word!

為什麼？你答應我的耶！

會話2

例 Sweetie, promise me you will not drive after you drink.

親愛的，答應我你不會酒後開車。

例 Yes, you have my word.

好的，我答應你。

track 059

我們要一起解決
We need to work this out.

解析

遇到問題的情侶最需要的就是兩個人一起共同解決囉！所以這時候就會說：We need to work this out. 就是我們必須要一起面對的意思。

會話 1

例 I do not have confidence about this long distance relationship.

我對於這段遠距離戀愛很沒有信心。

例 Babe, we need to work this out, and we will.

寶貝，我們會一起解決這個問題的。

會話 2

例 What do you think we should do, Mom?

媽，你覺得我們應該怎麼辦？

例 You're married. You two should work it out together.

你們已經結婚了，應該是你們兩個自己解決這個問題。

你到底在說什麼？

What are you talking about?

解 析

這裡比較有不可思議的感覺，覺得對方怎麼說這種話，而不是聽不清楚而問對方在說什麼。

會 話 1

例 You did not go out with Jeff last night, right?

你昨晚根本不是跟傑夫出去對不對？

例 What are you talking about?

你在說什麼？

會 話 2

例 She stole my wallet.

她偷了我的皮夾。

例 What are you talking about? She is your cousin!

你在說什麼啊，她是你表妹耶！

🎧 track 060

我很失控

I was not myself.

解析

當衝突過後除了說抱歉之外，像前面提到的太衝動：impulsive也可以說：我剛剛太失控了，很失態。

會話 1

例 I am sorry. I was not myself.

對不起，我剛剛很失控。

例 It's ok, I know you were really mad.

沒關係啦，我知道你剛剛真的很生氣。

會話 2

例 Did I say something bad to you last night?

我昨晚有說什麼很不好聽的話嗎？

④ 情人

例 Kind of. You were not yourself because you were so drunk.

有吧。你醉到我都認不出了。

你是獨一無二的
You are one of a kind.

解析

每個人都想當另一半眼裡最特別的人,這句話就可以用來表示,獨一無二的意思!也有:You are one in a million. 就是很多很多人裡,我只看到你。

會話 1

例 I do not know why you are so crazy about her.

我不知道你為什麼這麼為她瘋狂。

例 She is one of a kind.

她是獨一無二的。

會話 2

例 Do you think I am not skinny and beautiful?

你覺得我是不是不瘦也不美?

例 Don't be silly. You are one of a kind.
別傻了，你是最特別的。

🎧track 061

事情不是你想的那樣
It is not what you think it is.

解析

誤會最容易造成衝突及吵架了，而且有時候只看到事情的表面真的很容易誤解，所以這時就會說：It is not what you think it is. 事情不是只有你看到的那樣。

會話 1

例 I cannot believe you did that to me.
我不敢相信你會對我做出這樣的事。

例 It is not what you think it is.
事情不是你想的那樣。

會話 2

例 Why did you look so close with the guy in the photo?

為什麼照片中你和那個男生那麼親密的樣子？

例 It is not what you think it is. He is a very good friend of mine.

不是你想的那樣啦，他是我很好的一個朋友。

只是小事
It is not a big deal.

解 析

有時候吵架，有一方都會覺得是小事，不值得大動肝火甚至提出來講，於是就會說：It is not a big deal.「這又沒有什麼」。

會 話 1

例 Why did you teach him to play video games?

你為什麼要教他打電動？

例 It is not a big deal.

這又沒有什麼。

例 But he is only 4 years old.
但是他只有四歲。

會 話 2

例 Don't be upset. It is not a big deal.
不要不開心了,這只是小事啊。

例 No. It is a big deal.
對我來說是大事。

🎧 track 062

④
情
人

結束了
It is over.

解 析

除了用在一般日常生活,像是比賽、活動
或是表演。當一段感情結束的時候,就也
是說:It's over.

會 話 1

例 So what are you going to do?
所以你打算怎麼做?

例 I think it's over. I will break up with her.

我覺得已經結束了，我會跟她分手。

會話 **2**

例 It is over, Danny! Do not call me anymore!

我們之間結束了，丹尼！不要再打給我了！

例 No, it's not!

才沒有結束！

可以再給我一次機會嗎？
Can I have a second chance?

解 析

在做錯事情後，總是希望有第二次機會來彌補過失，這時候通常就會說：I need a second chance.

會話 **1**

例 I would never give him a second chance.

我絕對不會給他第二次機會。

例 Why?
為什麼？

會話 2

例 Please, can I have a second chance?
拜託，能再給我一次機會嗎？

例 I have given you a thousand chances.
我已經給你了一千個機會了。

track 063

我搞砸了
I screwed up.

解析

若是事情沒有做好、達到應有的標準，就會用：我搞砸了。在一段感情中，通常也會聽到人家這麼用。

會話 1

例 What happened? Why are you crying?
發生什麼事了？你怎麼在哭啊？

例 I screwed up. I cheated on her.

我搞砸了，我對不起她。

會話 2

例 Sorry, I screwed up.

對不起我搞砸了。

例 Never mind. We can fix it.

沒關係，我們可以解決的。

我在聽

I'm all ears.

解析

想說什麼就說啊，我就在這裡聽看看你要
說什麼。若是有人有話要說，這時候就可
以回答：我在聽啊，你可以說。

會話 1

例 I need to tell you something big.

我要跟你說一件很重要的事。

例 I'm all ears.

我在聽。

會話2

例 I have a great idea.
我有一個好主意。

例 I'm all ears.
我洗耳恭聽。

🎧 track 064

我反應太大了
I was overreacting.

④情人

解析

就是反應過度的意思,是很常用的一句話。只要有人為了小事而大動干戈,就可以用這句話。

會話1

例 I want to apologize.
我想要道歉。

例 For what?
哪件事?

例 I was overreacting to the news you are quitting your job.

我對你要辭職的事反應過大了些。

會話 2

例 How could you have dinner with her as soon as I left?

你怎麼可以在我走了之後馬上跟她吃飯？

例 She is just a friend. You are overreacting.

她只是個朋友，你反應過度了。

我幾乎不能呼吸

I can hardly breathe.

解析

如果是用在男女生之間，就是表示看到喜歡的人很緊張，都不能呼吸了。

會話 1

例 She is walking toward me.

她朝我這裡走來了。

例 So?

所以呢？

例 Oh dear, I can hardly breathe.

我的天啊，我不能呼吸了。

會話2

例 You look so nervous. What happened?

你看起來好緊張，怎麼了？

例 I can hardly breathe whenever she talks
to me.

每次她只要一跟我說話我就呼吸困難。

🎧 track 065

他/她不是我能高攀得上的

S / he is a little out of my league.

解 析

有時候對自己沒信心、覺得自己不夠好，
就會說一些自己配不上啊這類的話。

會話 1

例 Go! Go talk to her!
快去跟她講話啊！

例 I don't know. She is a little out of my league. She is a model!
我不知道耶，她可是模特兒，我想我是高攀不上。

會話 2

例 He is totally into you.
他真的喜歡你。

例 No way. He is tall, rich and handsome. He is competely out of my league.
不可能，他又高又有錢又帥，他完全不是我可以配得上的。

他為你瘋狂
He is mad about you.

解析

也就是他很喜歡你的意思，也可以說 He is so into you.

會話 1

例 He is mad about you.
他為你瘋狂了。

例 Really? I don't know.
有嗎？我不知道。

會話 2

例 I am so mad about her.
我好喜歡她哦。

例 Then you should at least try to talk to her.
那你至少也得試著跟她說句話吧。

4 情人

小·叮·嚀

> 另一個mad用法是mad at someone意思是對某人生氣，跟mad about完全不一樣意思哦！

track 066

完全超出我的期待
It was beyond all expectations.

解析

所預期的事物如果是超出期待就是 beyond，那如果是不符期待呢？就可以用 fall short of來表示囉。

會話 1

例 How was your vacation?
你的假期如何？

例 It was beyond all expectations.
完全超出我的期待。

會話 2

例 The trip totally fell short of expectations.
這趟旅遊完全就是不符合期待。

例 I feel sorry for you.
很遺憾。

我必須鼓起勇氣

I must pluck up the courage.

解析

鼓起勇氣去做某件事可以用 pluck up the courage 來表示,所以下次鼓勵別人或是自己的時候就可以這樣說囉。

會話 1

例 I must pluck up the courage to ask her to marry me.

我必須鼓起勇氣跟她求婚。

例 Everything will be fine.

一切都會順利的。

會話 2

例 I just can't pluck up the courage to tell him the truth.

我就是無法鼓起勇氣跟他說事情的真相。

例 But he will find out sooner or later.

但是他遲早會知道的。

4
情
人

Chapter

5

學校

我快要爆炸了
I am dying!

解析

報告、作業、考試太多了，堆滿滿的，感覺就快爆炸了一樣，這時候可以說：我被逼得快死掉了！

會話 **1**

例 I am dying!
我快要死了！

例 Why?
為什麼？

例 I have four exams in one week!
我一個禮拜要考四科！

❺ 學校

會話 **2**

例 I did not sleep last night. I'm dying.
我昨晚都沒有睡，我要死掉了。

例 Yeah, I can see that.
是啊，看的出來。

功課也太多了
Too much homework!

解析

學生最常抱怨回家作業太多,這時候就可以用 too much homework. 因為 homework 是不可數的,所以用 much。

會話 1

例 I really want to go, but I can't. I got too much homework to do.

我真的很想跟你去,可是我有好多功課要做。

例 All right, that is too bad.

好吧,太可惜了。

會話 2

例 Oh my god! Too much homework for the weekend! I want to play!

我的天啊,這週末有太多功課了啦!我想出去玩!

例 Tell me about it.

可不是嗎。

這堂課也太早了
This class is way too early.

解析

如果是在能夠選課的情況下，譬如在大學。有時候很早的課都是必修，雖然不想修，可是又沒有辦法，大家就會一起抱怨說，這堂課也太早了。

會話1

例 Are you sure that you want to take that class?

你確定你要修那堂課嗎？

例 It looks interesting.

它感覺很有趣的樣子

例 I know, but it is way too early.

是沒錯，可是也太早了吧

會話2

例 It is way too early. I don't want to take it and not be able to attend it.

課真的太早了，我不想選了然後都不去

例 True.

也是。

幫我抄筆記

Can you take notes for me?

解析

同學之間最常互相幫忙的事，不外乎就是
抄筆記了，如果有事無法上課聽講，就可
以請求有上課的同學幫忙記一下老師上課
的重點囉！

會話 1

例 Can you take notes for me later?

你等一下可以幫我記一下筆記嗎？

例 Sure.

好啊。

會話 2

例 You cannot keep taking notes for him.
He does not even come to class!

你不能再幫他抄筆記了啦，他根本都不來
上課！

例 I don't know how to say no.
　我不知道該怎麼拒絕啊。

🎧 track 069

我可以跟你借筆記嗎

Can I borrow your notes?

解析

若因有事請假而沒有抄到上課筆記，又忘記請同學幫忙抄，這時候就只好借同學的來看一下了。

會話 **1**

例 Can I borrow your notes?
　我可以跟你借一下筆記嗎？

例 Of course.
　當然可以。

會話 **2**

例 Do you need my notes?
　你需要看我的筆記嗎？

例 Can I? Thanks a lot!
　可以嗎？太感謝你了！

我毫無頭緒

I have no idea. / I don't have a clue.

解 析

遇到不知該如何回答，或是不知該怎麼解決的事情，除了說I don't know. 之外，也可以用這句I have no idea. 或是I don't have a clue.來表示。

會 話 1

例 Do you know who is going to be our new history teacher?

你知道誰會是我們新的歷史老師嗎？

例 I have no idea.

我毫無頭緒。

會 話 2

例 What is wrong with me? Am I sick? I feel horrible.

我是怎麼了，生病了嗎？我感到很糟。

例 I don't have a clue. Maybe you should go to a doctor.

我也不曉得，你還是去看一下醫生好了。

我死定了

I am done for.

解析

若是功課忘記完成、東西忘記帶，或是考試沒準備好等等的情況，覺得自己一定會被老師教訓一頓，就可以說：我死定了。

會話 1

例 I am done for.

我死定了。

例 Why?

怎麼會？

例 I forgot to print it out.

我忘記印出來了。

會話 2

例 Did Mr. Lee say we have to read these pages yesterday?

李老師昨天有說我們要先讀這幾頁嗎？

例 Yup, he did.

有啊，他有說。

❺
學
校

例 I am done for.

　那我死定了。

根本不算糟啊

It wasn't half bad at all.

解 析

有時候如果別人遇到麻煩，除了可以幫忙解決之外，也可以說一些讓對方可以不要那麼著急的話，像這句就可以派得上用場。

會 話 1

例 See, I told you Dr. Cooper hates me. I only got a B.

　看吧，我就說Dr. Cooper 討厭我，我只拿了 B。

例 Come on. It wasn't half bad at all. We all got a B.

　拜託，根本不會很爛好嗎，我們大家都是 B。

會 話 2

例 Crap, my powerpoint sucks.

　天啊，我的投影片糟透了。

例 It isn't half bad at all. You just need to add an outline and everything will be fine.

這不會很糟，你只是需要加一張大綱就會看起來更好了。

track 071

放輕鬆！
Relax!

解析

有很多情況，譬如說要考試或是報告時都會容易緊張，這時候除了告訴別人要放輕鬆，也可以跟自己說。

會話 1

例 Today is my first day of college.
今天是我大學的第一天。

例 Relax! It is going to be great!
放輕鬆！一切都會很好的！

會話 2

例 You need to relax!
你真的需要放輕鬆一點！

例 I can't. I have never delivered a speech in front of 300 people.
我無法，我從來沒有在 300 人面前演講過。

說的好！

Good point!

解析

算是認同對方所說的話，如果是 Good idea. 就是好主意的意思。

會話 1

例 Maybe you are just too tired. Go home and rest then you will be fine.
也許你只是太累了，回家休息就會好了啦。

例 Good point.
沒錯，說的對。

會話 2

例 After we finish our homework, maybe we can go to see a movie?

也許我們也可以在寫完作業後去看個電影？

例 Good idea!

好主意！

🎧track 072

你人真好
It is so kind of you.

解析

若有人幫忙自己，或是好人好事代表，就可以跟對方說他人真好來表示自己的青睞，kind也可以用nice。

會話 1

例 Here, this is the note from the math class.

拿去，這是數學課的筆記。

迷你短句

例 Thank you! It is so kind of you!
　謝謝你！你人真好！

會話 2

例 Martin fixed my laptop yesterday!
　馬汀昨天幫我把筆電修好了！

例 It is so nice of him!
　他人真好！

他/她只是在拍馬屁
S / he is trying to butter you up.

解析

這句話可以用在同學和老師之間，也可以有很多其它的情況可使用，譬如上司與下屬、親子之間等等，為了討好某人而說的好聽話。

會話 1

例 Do not listen to him. He is trying to butter you up.
你不要聽他的，他只是想拍你馬屁。

例 So what does he want from me?
那他究竟想從我這裡得到什麼？

會話 2

例 She is always trying to butter Miss Lin up.
她總是想拍Miss Lin的馬屁。

例 And Miss Lin seems to enjoy it.
而Miss Lin看起來也很享受啊。

🎧 track 073

我不認為哦
I don't think so.

解析

這句話其實是非常的好用，在日常生活中只要遇到不是百分之百認同的情況、想法或是行為，都可以說I don't think so.

會話 1

例 I think Mr. Lee is the most handsome teacher in the school.
我覺得李老師是全校最帥的老師了。

例 I don't think so.
我不這麼認為耶。

會話 2

例 Who wants to study history? It is useless.
誰會想唸歷史啊,根本沒有用。

例 I don't think so. It is really useful.
我不這樣認為,我覺得很有幫助啊。

這就是我知道的
That is all I got.

解析

意思就是說:我所知道的、我所能提供的就是這些了,再多就沒有了。

會話 1

例 Tell me more about her ex-boyfriend.
再跟我說多一點她前男友的事。

例 That is all I got.
我所知道的就這些了。

會話 2

例 Can you speak French?

你會說法文嗎？

例 Bonjour, bonsoir. That's all I got.

早安，晚安，就這樣。

track 074

沒有什麼特別的
Nothing important.

解析

與之前提過的nothing special有些類似，
都是指沒有什麼重要或是特別的事發生。

5 學校

會話 1

例 Did Mr. Lee say anything in class yesterday?

李老師昨天上課有說什麼嗎？

例 No, nothing important.

沒有什麼特別重要的。

會話 2

例 How was the swimming class this morning?

今天早上的游泳課還好嗎？

例 Cool, nothing important.

還好啊，沒什麼特別的。

沒問題

By all means.

解析

其實by all means最常看到的意思是：盡一切力量去做、去完成。但是後來也有引申為sure，也就是沒問題啊、好啊的意思。

會話 1

例 Can you tell Miss Lin that I am sick today?

你可以幫我跟Miss Lin說我今天生病嗎？

例 By all means.

沒問題。

會話 2

例 We need to finish this task by all means.
我們無論如何一定要完成這個任務。

例 We can do it.
我們可以的。

🎧 track 075

懂了嗎？(懂了)
Got it? (Got it.)

解析

問別人懂了嗎通常會想到Do you under-
stand? 但是有點太長了，所以可以問對方
Got it? 如果對方認為沒問題，就能回答
Got it.

會話 1

例 All we need to do is to put the pie
into the oven, got it?
我們所需要做的就是把派放進烤箱就好，
懂了嗎？

例 Got it!

懂了！

會話 2

例 You have to finish the paper before next Wednesday, got it?

你們必須在下星期三之前完成報告，可以嗎？

例 Got it.

知道了。

想都別想

Not on your life.

解 析

有「絕對不行」、「想都別想」的意思，若是有人提出什麼太超過的要求，就可以說 Not on your life!

會話 1

例 Do you think that I can ask Mr. Lee to postpone the deadline?

你覺得我可以去拜託李老師延後繳交期限嗎?

例 Not on your life.
想都別想。

會話 2

例 Can I borrow your laptop?
你可以借我你的筆電嗎?

例 Not on your life.
絕對不行。

 ⓝtrack 076

你不是認真的吧
You can't be serious.

解 析

事情已經荒謬到了無法置信的地步,這時就像之前提過的「你在開玩笑嗎?Are you kidding me?」或是 seriously?

會話 1

例 Mr. Lee said yes to my request.
李老師答應了我的請求

❺
學
校

例 You can't be serious.
你不是認真的吧。

會話 2

例 I have decided to go to India for six months.
我決定要去印度六個月。

例 What? You can't be serious!
什麼？你不是認真的吧！

我求求你了

I am begging you.

解析

懇求、拜託的口氣，常常會聽到有人說：
拜託拜託我求求你。除了說please之外還
可以加強語氣說：I'm begging you!

會話 1

例 I don't have time to help you with your presentation.
我沒有時間幫你準備你的報告。

例 Please, I'm begging you.
　拜託，求求你啦。

會話 **2**

例 I'm begging you.
　求求你。

例 Not on your life.
　想都沒想。

🎧track 077

真丟臉

Shame on you.

解 析

這句話如果認真的說會覺得很嚴重，感覺
是：你真可恥。不過越來越變成只是開開
玩笑的說。

會話 **1**

例 I hit my neighbor's dog.
　我撞到我鄰居的狗。

例 Shame on you.
　你真可惡。

5
學
校

會話 2

例 Did I just drool on the desk?

我剛剛流口水流到桌子上嗎？

例 Shame on you.

真丟臉。

我有點搞混了
I am a little confused.

解 析

這句話的意思是：有點搞混了、有些不明白。在很多情況之下都非常好用。

會話 1

例 I am a little confused. Aren't you my friend's girlfriend?

我有點搞混了，你不是我朋友的女朋友嗎？

例 Oh, we are twins.

哦，我們是雙胞胎啦。

會話 2

例 The deadline has been postponed to the end of this month, right?
繳交期延到這個月底對嗎？

例 I don't know. I'm a little confused.
我不知道耶，有點搞混了。

🎧 track 078

這不關你的事
It is none of your business.

解析

當有人問太多或是管太多的時候，就可以用這句話表示，這不干你的事，可以不用這麼熱心啦！

會話 1

例 Have you heard that Miss Lin broke up with her boyfriend?
你有聽說林老師和他男朋友分手了嗎？

例 It is none of my business, so I don't want to know.

這不關我的事，我不想知道。

會話 2

例 How was your final?

期末考的如何啊？

例 It is none of your business.

不關你的事啦。

這並沒有錯

I found nothing wrong.

解析

這句話的意思就是：我不覺得哪裡有錯啊、這並不奇怪啊等等。

會話 1

例 Are you sure about the answer to this question?

你確定這題的答案嗎？

例 I found nothing wrong.
我不認為哪裡有錯。

會話 **2**

例 I found nothing wrong with that.
這沒有錯啊。

例 But it is a little strange, don't you think?
可是這有點奇怪啊你不覺得嗎？

∩ track 079

這不是我的強項
It is not my strong suit.

解 析

It 可以替換成任何東西，數學、跳舞、英文、體育啊等等的，用來表示真的不是很擅長從事一些活動或是某些科目。

會話 **1**

例 You should go dancing with us.
你應該跟我們去跳舞。

例 It is really not my strong suit.
跳舞真的不是我的強項。

會話 2

例 Let's cook for mom tonight!
我們今晚為媽媽煮飯吧！

例 Cooking is not my strong suit.
下廚可不是我的強項。

祝你好運
Good luck.

解析

其實現在最常用的祝你好運是用：Break a leg. 字面上好像是摔斷腿，但是意思是祝你好運、祝你有好的表現的意思。

會話 1

例 My interview is next Friday.
我的面試是下週五。

例 Go break a leg!
祝你好運！

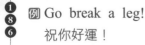

會話 2

例 When is your performance?
你什麼時候表演？

例 Tomorrow!
明天！

例 Break a leg!
祝你好運！

🎧 track 080

你是告密的人！
You are a rat!

❺
學
校

解析

rat是老鼠，感覺像是鼠輩，用來表示像鼠輩一樣告密的人。

會話 1

例 You are a rat!
你根本就是告密者！

例 I did not say anything!
我什麼都沒有説！

會話 2

例 You are a rat.
你是個告密者。

例 It is for your own good.
這都是為了你好。

我會轉交的
I will pass it on.

解析

意指將東西或是訊息轉交給他人。

會話 1

例 Can you tell Sally that the meeting is at 9 o'clock tomorrow morning?
你可以跟莎莉說明天早上九點開會嗎？

例 I will pass it on.
我會幫你告訴她的。

會話 2

例 Can you help me hand in my paper to Dr. Cooper?

你可以幫我把報告交給Dr. Cooper嗎？

例 Sure, I will pass it on.

沒問題，我會轉交給他的。

 ∩ track 081

我忘得一乾二淨！
I totally forgot!

解析

使用時有驚呼表示完全忘記有這件事存在。

會話 1

例 Yesterday was Dad's birthday. Where were you?

昨天是爸爸的生日，你在哪啊？

例 What? I totally forgot!

什麼！我完全忘記了！

會話 2

例 We will have a quiz today.
今天有一個小考。

例 Really? I totally forgot.
真的嗎？我忘得一乾二淨耶。

他請病假

S / he is on sick leave.

解 析

上課上班難免會因為生病而請假，如果需要別人幫忙請假的時候，就可以使用這句話囉！

會話 1

例 Is Kyle here today?
凱爾今天有來嗎？

例 Mr. Lee, he is on sick leave.
李老師，他今天請病假。

會話 2

例 Too bad she is on sick leave today.

她今天請病假真是太可惜了。

例 Yeah, the movie we saw in class was really great.

對啊,課堂上看的電影真的很棒耶。

🎧 track 082

你下課多久?

How long is your break?

解析

除了是在一般國高中學校,是一整天都要上課,大學以上在課與課之間有可能會有很長的空白時間是沒有課的,所以有時候就會問對方這句話,看對方中間下課有多久。

會話 1

例 How long is your break? Do you want a cup of coffee?

你下課多久?想喝杯咖啡嗎?

5 學校

例 I have two hours, let's go.
我有兩個小時,走吧。

會話 2

例 I want to discuss with you tomorrow's
presentation with you.
我想跟你討論一下明天的報告。

例 Ok, see you at my break time.
好的,下課見。

你明天有課嗎?
Do you have class tomorrow?

解析
這句話有可能是同學之間互相詢問,也有
可能是問老師,用在老師身上就是問他有
沒有要教的課啊?

會話 1

例 Do you have class tomorrow?
你明天有課嗎?

例 Yes, Research Methods.
有啊,研究方法。

會 話 2

例 I do not have class tomorrow. Do you want to go to a movie?

我明天沒有課,你想去看個電影嗎?

例 But I do.

可是我有課。

🎧track 083

我不翹課的

I never skip class.

解 析

愛翹課的同學會影響其他人跟他一起翹課,好學生這時候就可以說:我從不翹課的哦!

會 話 1

例 Hey, let's hang out tomorrow. The history class is boring anyway.

嘿,我們明天出去玩吧,反正歷史課很無聊。

例 Thanks for asking, but I never skip class.

謝謝你的邀請，但是我不翹課的。

會話 2

例 Can you be a bad student for once? Just skip the class.

你就不能當一次壞學生翹課一下嗎？

例 Are you sure that it will be ok?

你確定會沒事嗎？

我覺得很丟臉

I feel embarrassed.

解析

如果發生什麼很丟臉、尷尬的事，或是感到實在很窘就可以這樣說。

會話 1

例 Can you stop doing this?

你可以停止嗎？

例 Why? I'm just singing.

為什麼？我只是在唱歌。

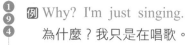

例 I feel embarrassed.

我覺得很丟臉耶。

會話 2

例 It was embarrassing to see your mom drunk.

看到你媽喝醉超尷尬的。

例 Sorry about that.

很不好意思。

🎧 track 084

我欠你一次

I owe you one.

解 析

欠人家就是用 owe，所以當別人幫自己忙的時候呢，就可以說我欠你一次囉。

會話 1

例 Can you pick me up at the airport next Tuesday, please?

你可以下星期二來機場接我嗎，拜託？

例 Ok…, but you owe me one.
好吧…，但你欠我一次哦。

會話 2

例 Do I really have to go with you?
我真的一定要跟你去嗎？

例 Please!
拜託啦！

例 Ok.
好吧。

例 Yay! I owe you one.
耶！我欠你一次啦。

我想是吧

I suppose so.

解 析

有猜想、以為、假設的語氣，之前有提到
一個 I guess so. 但是這裡 suppose 猜測的
意味更少一些，有「認定應該是怎麼樣」
的意思。

會話1

例 We should hand in the paper before Friday, shouldn't we?

我們應該是要在星期五之前交報告對吧？

例 I suppose so.

我想是吧。

會話2

例 Where is Daniel?

你有看到丹尼爾嗎？

例 I suppose he is still in the lab.

我想他應該還在實驗室。

🎧track 085

我拼命唸書

I throw myself into my studies.

解析

Throw 是丟，把自己丟進某個狀況裡，就是 throw oneself into something. 所以如果自己是完全認真的在唸書就可以這樣表示囉。

會話 1

例 I think it's time to throw myself into my studies.

我想是時候來拼個命唸書了。

例 I'm glad that you have this idea just one day before your exam.

我很欣慰在考試前一天你有這樣的想法。

會話 2

例 Where have you been? I couldn't reach you for the past few weeks.

你去了哪裡啊？我好幾個禮拜找不到你。

例 I threw myself into my studies.

我在努力唸書啊。

他只是在戲弄你

He is just teasing you.

解 析

有挑逗、取笑、戲弄的意思，通常是比較開玩笑不是認真的。

會話 1

例 Why is he so annoying?

他為什麼要這麼討厭？

例 Ignore him; he is just teasing you.

不要理他，他只是鬧著你玩的。

會話 2

例 If you tease that dog, he might bite you.

如果你戲弄那隻狗，牠可能會咬你哦。

例 I'm not teasing him. I'm just trying to
play with him.

我沒有在戲弄牠啊，我只是想跟牠玩。

我會試著搞清楚的

I will try to figure it out.

解 析

有理解、想清楚的意思，所以遇到難題或
是難懂的人，就可以用這個來表示。

會話 1

例 Why can't I figure this out!

為什麼我這個就是搞不懂！

例 It's not that hard. Calm down.

沒有那麼難，冷靜想一下。

會話 2

例 There is something in this story, so you need to read it carefully.

故事裡蘊藏著某些含意，你必須細細品味。

例 Ok, I will try to figure it out.

好的，我會試解理解。

MORNING ROUTINE

 LEMON WATER

 FITNESS

 SHOWER

 BEAUTY ROUTINE

 BREAKFAST

Chapter

6

電話

我需要打通電話

I need to make a phone call.

解 析

當需要打個電話的時候該怎麼說呢？其實大部份的說法就是這樣，而且大部份的外國人講重要的電話都會先說這句，然後再走到旁邊去打，比較禮貌。

會 話

例 I need to make a phone call.
我需要打通電話。

例 Ok, I'll be waiting by the car.
好的，我去車子那邊等你。
@會話：

例 Do you need me to make a phone call to your parents?
你需要我幫你打個電話給你父母嗎？

例 No, I don't want them to be worried.
不用，我不想他們擔心。

我需要接電話

I need to get this.

解析

有時候在一場合不方便接電話,也不會接
電話,可是看到來電顯示是重要的電話有
時候就會失禮的說:不好意思,我必須接
個電話。

會話

例 I need to get this.

我需要接這通電話。

例 But you are driving. Can't you call
back later?

但是你在開車,不能待會再回撥嗎?

例 It's my boss.

是我老闆打的。

例 Ok, pull over then.

好吧,那靠邊停。

我就是

Speaking.

解析

在電話裡切記千萬不可以說我就是說成：
I am XXX.哦！要說This is XXX. 或是直
接說Speaking.

會話1

例 May I speak to Rose?
我找蘿絲？

例 Speaking.
我就是。

會話2

例 May I speak to Mandy?
我找曼蒂？

例 This is Mandy.
我就是。

6
電
話

我可以留言嗎？
Can I leave a message?

解析

若你在電話中要找的人不在，不是急事的話就可以請接電話的人留個言，就是用 leave a message.

會話 1

例 She is still sleeping.

她還在睡覺。

例 Can I leave a message?

我可以留言嗎？

會話 2

例 I do not want to take the phone call. Can you ask him to leave a message?

我現在不想接電話，你可以請他留言嗎？

例 Ok, no problem.

好的，沒問題。

⏺ track 088

我幫你轉接

Let me put you through.

解析

通常在幫別人轉接電話至其它線路時，就可以這樣說。

會話 1

例 Let me put you through.
我幫你轉接。

例 Thank you.
謝謝。

會話 2

例 Could you put me through?
你可以幫我轉接嗎？

例 Hold on.
請稍等。

🎧 track 089

請稍等

Hold on.

解析

這就時常聽到囉，Hang on的意思也是與之雷同，都有請稍等一下的意思，尤其是在電話中，更是要這樣說，也可以加 a minute 或是 a moment。

會話1

例 May I speak to James?
　請找詹姆士？

例 Hold on a moment please.
　請稍等一下。

會話2

例 Put your brother on the phone.
　叫你哥哥來聽電話。

例 Hold on.
　等一下哦。

我找⋯

May I speak to ⋯.
(I'd like to talk to⋯)

解析

在前面幾句都有提到，因為只是在電話中
找人，這樣講就沒錯了。

會話 **1**

例 Hello, may I speak to Mr. Wang, please.
哈囉，請找王先生。

例 Wait a moment please.
請稍等一下。

會話 **2**

例 I'd like to talk to Mrs. Lin.
我找林太太。

例 Let me put you through.
我幫你轉接。

是什麼事？

What is the matter?

解析

有些環境或是人會有先過濾電話的習慣，
這時候就會說：請問是有什麼事嗎？

會話1

例 May I speak to Peter?

我找彼得。

例 He is in the shower. What is the matter?

他在洗澡，請問有什麼事嗎？

會話2

例 I will call you back.

我待會回電。

例 Who is it? What is the matter?

是誰打的，是什麼事啊？

例 Sam asked me what today's homework is.

山姆問我今天的功課是什麼。

我需要你的幫忙
I need your help.

解析

有時候打電話給人求助，這句話就很好用啦。

會話1

例 Hello?
喂？

例 Peter, it's me, Sam. I need your help.
彼得，我是山姆，我需要你的幫忙。

會話2

例 Hello? Cindy? I need your help!
喂？辛蒂，我需要你的幫忙！

例 Slow down, who are you?
等等，你是誰啊？

下次聊
Talk soon.

解析

要說再見時，也可以用下次聊來結束，還有 Talk to you later. 也可以說哦。

會話 1

例 Good night.

晚安。

例 Talk soon.

下次聊。

會話 2

例 Ok, I need to go to class.

嗯，我該去上課了。

例 Sure, talk to you later.

好，下次再聊。

我會轉告他你的來電

I'll tell her / him you called.

解析

整句話是 I will tell her/him that you called. 講快一些就會像是 I'll tell her/him you called. 如不留言，就轉告當事者。

會話 1

例 Do you need to leave a message?
你需要留言嗎？

例 No, it's fine, just tell her I called.
沒關係不用了，跟她說我有打來就好。

會話 2

例 I will tell him you called.
我會轉告他你的來電。

例 Thank you very much.
非常感謝你。

6
電話

這是 xxx 的回電
This is xxx returning your call.

解 析

有時候回電話並不一定知道剛剛打來的是
誰，這時就可以說，這是某某某回電，請
問剛剛有人打電話找我嗎？

會話 1

例 This is Peter returning your call.
這是彼得回電。

例 May I have your last name please?
可以請您告訴我您的姓氏嗎？

例 Chen, Peter Chen.
我姓陳。

例 Hold on a second.
請稍等一下。

會話 2

例 Hello? This is Jenny returning your
call. Did anyone call this number?

哈囉，這是珍妮回電，請問剛剛有人打這支電話嗎？

例 Hi, Jenny! It's Sandy!
嗨，珍妮！我是珊迪啦！

🎧 track 092

我能幫你嗎？
How may I help you?

解析

接到朋友請求協助的電話，該怎麼回答呢？就可以說，我能怎麼樣幫你呢？或是直接一點的意思是：請問有什麼事嗎？

會話1

例 Hello, Jane. Am I bothering you?
喂，珍，我有吵到你嗎？

例 Not at all. How may I help you?
不會不會，有什麼事嗎？

會話 2

例 This is the customer service line, how may I help you?

這是顧客服務專線,請問有什麼需要協助的地方呢?

例 Can I talk to your manager?

我可以找經理嗎?

你現在方便說話嗎?

Are you free to talk?

解析

打電話給別人比較有禮貌的話會先問對方有沒有空、方便說話嗎?

會話 1

例 Hello?

喂?

例 Mary, this is Louis. Are you free to talk?

瑪莉,我是路易,你現在方便說話嗎?

會話 2

例 Hello, are you free to talk now?

喂，你現在方便說話嗎？

例 I am driving. Can I call you back later?

我在開車，待會打給你好嗎？

 track 093

我再打給你

I will call you back.

解 析

如同前述所提及的，若是沒有辦法現在處理來電，則會告知對方待會再撥給他哦。

會話 1

例 Can you talk right now?

你現在可以講話嗎？

例 I am in a meeting. I will call you back.

我在開會，待會打給你。

6
電
話

會話 2

例 Hello? Hello?

喂？喂？

例 I am running out of battery, I will call you back.

我電池沒電了，再打給你。

謝謝你打來
Thanks for the call.

解析

一通電話不管是祝賀還是關心都會讓人感到溫暖，這時候就可以用到這句話囉。

會話 1

例 Happy birthday, Christina!

克莉絲汀生日快樂！

例 Hey! Thanks for the call!

嘿！謝謝你打來！

會話 2

例 How are you holding up? Your mom is in the hospital. It must be tough.

你還好嗎？媽媽住院對你來説一定很辛苦。

例 Yeah, I'm doing fine. Thanks for the call.

是啊，我還可以啦，謝謝你的關心。

track 094

你可以大聲/慢一點嗎？

Could you please speak louder /slower?

解析

若是手機收訊不好或是其它原因，在電話中聽不清楚對方的聲音，要請對方大聲或是慢一點的時候，就可以這樣説。

會話1

例 Could you please speak louder?

你可以講大聲一點嗎？

例 I can't. My dad is sleeping next door.

不行，我爸在我隔壁睡覺。

會話 2

例 Do you get it?

你懂了嗎？

例 I'm sorry, could you say that again and speak slower?

很抱歉，可以請你再說一次並講慢一點嗎？

我聽不太清楚

I cannot hear you well.

解 析

如同前述提到，聽不清楚對方的聲音時，就可以說：我聽不清楚！可以再講一次嗎？I cannot hear you. 或是Can you repeat one more time?

會話 1

例 I cannot hear you well. Where are you?

我聽不太清楚，你人在哪啊？

例 I am at the night market!

我在夜市。

會話 2

例 I can hear you well, so you don't need to shout.

我聽的很清楚，你不必大喊。

例 Oh, sorry.

哦，不好意思。

🎧 track 095

你可以再打一次嗎？
Could you call again?

解析

當要請對方再撥一次過來時，記得電話裡的禮貌不可少，用 could 比用 can 好一些哦！

6
電話

會話 1

例 She will be back in 1 hour, could you call again?

她一小時後回來，你可以到時再打一次嗎？

例 Ok, thank you very much.

好的，謝謝你。

會話 2

例 No one answered.

沒有人接啊。

例 Could you call again?

你再打一次嘛?

他現在不在

S / he is not in.

解析

除了說幫你轉接之外,那若是對方要找的人不在位子上,就可以簡單的說:She or he is not in.

會話 1

例 May I speak to Amy?

我找艾咪

例 She is not in. Do you want to leave a message?

她不在,你需要留言嗎?

例 Oh, it's ok. Just tell her I called. I'm Ted.
哦,沒關係,請轉告她我有來電,我是泰德。

會話2

例 Mr. Adams' office, how may I help you?
經理辦公室您好,請問您有什麼事嗎?

例 This is Dr. Cooper calling, may I speak to Mr. Adams?
這是Dr.Cooper,請問可以幫我接經理嗎?

例 I'm sorry, he's not in today.
很抱歉,他今天不在。

🎧 track 096

我會幫你轉接給…
I will transfer your call to….

解 析

與Let me put you through. 都可以一起使用,都是轉接的意思。

會話 1

例 I will transfer your call to the principal.

我幫你轉接到校長室。

例 Thank you very much.

非常謝謝你。

會話 2

例 I will transfer your call to someone who is in charge.

我會幫你轉接給負責的人員。

例 Yes, please.

好的,謝謝。

不接你電話嗎?

Not taking your call?

解 析

若是一直打一直打對方都不接電話,難免會擔心,這時旁邊是熟人看到了,不妨會關心一下。

會話1

例 Still not taking your call?
還是不接你電話嗎？

例 Yeah, it's been five days.
是啊，已經五天了。

會話2

例 I am mad because you did not take my call.
我生氣，因為你沒有接電話。

例 I am sorry, I did not carry my phone with me.
對不起，我的電話沒有帶在身上。

 track 097

我該怎麼辦？
What am I supposed to do?

解析

這句話不管是在電話中還是一般生活上，都會常常使用到，若是遇到棘手的情況，

難免會求助或是感到無奈，這時候就會常
說：What am I supposed to do?

會話 1

例 He is still not answering your call?
他還不是不接你電話嗎？

例 What am I supposed to do? He is so
mad at me.
我該怎麼辦，他在還生氣。

會話 2

例 What am I supposed to do?
我該怎麼做才好？

例 You should call 911.
你應該打給救護車。

他忙線中

Her / His line is busy now.

解 析

打電話或是要轉接的時候，對方不在，是
不在位子上還是忙線呢？這裡就讓大家知
道忙線的話可以怎麼說。

會話 1

例 This is Anna, may I speak to Mr. Chen?
我是安娜,請找陳先生。

例 Let me put you through. I am sorry, his line is busy now.
我幫你轉接。抱歉,他在忙線中。

會話 2

例 Hi, could you transfer me to Lisa?
嗨,你可以幫我轉給麗莎嗎?

例 Her line is busy now.
她在忙線中。

例 Ok, I will call back later.
好的,我待會再打。

🎧 track 098

無人接聽

The number you called /dialed is not available now.

解析

除了有忙線、不在位子上等等的說法，還有撥的電話響了很久沒人接聽的情況，這樣的說法就可以熟悉一下囉。

會話1

例 (The number you dialed is not available now, please leave a message or…)
您撥的電話沒有人回應，請留言或是……

例 I think he turned his cell phone off.
我想他應該是沒開機。

例 Try his house.
試試家裡的電話。

會話2

例 Did you make the reservation?
你訂位了嗎？

例 I couldn't. The line is not available.
還沒啊，電話沒有人接。

電話沒電了

My battery is dead.

解析

電池沒電了要怎麼說呢？除了用 run out (用盡)之外，也可以直接說電池死掉了！

會話 1

例 I can't hear you well!

我聽不清楚！

例 My battery is dead!

我的電話沒電了！

會話 2

例 Do you have a charger?

你有充電器嗎？

例 Running out of battery?

沒電了嗎？

🎧 track 099

我開振動

It is on vibrate mode.

解析

在一些需將手機關機的場合，有時候會開靜音或是振動，所以很難察覺有來電，這時候就能這樣解釋囉。

會話 1

例 Why did you not pick up my calls?
你為什麼沒有接我電話？

例 It was on vibrate mode.
我那時開振動沒聽到。

會話 2

例 Turn your cell to mute mode.
把電話轉靜音。

例 I will just turn it off.
我直接關機就好了。

你的鈴聲很好/難聽

Your ring tone rocks/sucks.

解析

講到手機,就會有鈴聲囉,如果遇到朋友的鈴聲很好聽或是很吵很難聽,該怎麼説呢?

會話 1

例 Your ring tone rocks. Where did you get it?

你的鈴聲很酷耶,在哪下載的?

例 I made it by myself.

我自己剪的。

會話 2

例 Your ring tone sucks. It sounds like a lullaby.

你的鈴聲很難聽耶,好像催眠曲。

例 I like it!

我很喜歡啊!

6
電話

🎧 track 100

可以傳簡訊給我嗎？
Could you text me?

解析

若是遇到不方便講電話的場合，但是可以允許用簡訊來聯絡，或是資訊太多無法一次記下，這時就可以跟對方說：可以用傳簡訊的嗎？

會話 1

例 Ok, here is the address of the restaurant.
這是餐廳的地址。

例 Could you text me?
你可以用傳簡訊的嗎？

會話 2

例 Are you free to talk now?
你現在方便說話嗎？

例 Not really, but you can text me.
不太能，但是你可以傳簡訊給我。

收訊很差

The reception is awful.

解析

不管是用在網路設備還是電話上，都可以表示收訊很不好哦。

會話1

例 The reception is awful. I can barely hear you.

收訊很差，我聽不到你的聲音。

例 Let me try again.

我再試撥一次。

會話2

例 How come the reception is so bad?

為什麼收訊這麼差？

例 Because we are in the middle of nowhere!

因為我們在一個很荒蕪的地方！

我們可以視訊啊

We can do a video call.

解析

通常一講到視訊通話，大部份的人都會想到 Skype，是許多私人或是商業的通訊軟體，所以其實很多人都會直接說：We can Skype.

會話 1

例 It will be expensive if you call me.
你打給我的話會很貴的。

例 No, we can Skype.
不會啊，我們可以用視訊通話。

會話 2

例 A long distance relationship is not easy.
遠距離戀愛很不容易的。

例 It's OK, we can do video calls, right?
還好啦，我們可以視訊啊，對不對？

我正在講電話！

I am on the phone!

解 析

常常遇到一些情況是，別人不知道你在講
電話，還不斷一直叫你，影響到你通話的
過程，這時候就會大喊：我在講電話啦！

會話 1

例 Linda! Dinner is ready! Linda? Linda!
琳達！晚餐準備好囉！琳達？琳達！

例 Ok! Mom! I am on the phone!
媽，我知道了！我正在講電話！

會話 2

例 What is your sister doing?
你妹妹在幹嘛？

例 She is on the phone.
她在講電話。

越快越好

As soon as possible.

解析

做什麼事、回什麼電話，很急很急的話就會跟對方說：越快越好。

會話1

例 I can't talk now; I am riding a bike.
我現在不方便說話，我在騎腳踏車。

例 Ok, call me back later, as soon as possible!
好，待會打給我，越快越好！

會話2

例 I will be there as soon as possible.
我會盡快到那邊的。

例 Thank you.
謝謝你。

MORNING ROUTINE

 LEMON WATER

 FITNESS

 SHOWER

 BEAUTY ROUTINE

 BREAKFAST

Chapter

7

吃飯

🎧 track 102

我餓了
I am starving.

解析

好餓好餓該怎麼說呢？除了說I am hungry.
通常英文都是用I am starving.來形容自己
很餓了。

會話 1

例 What's for dinner? I'm starving!
晚餐吃什麼，我餓死了！

例 Dumplings!
吃水餃！

會話 2

例 I am starving.
我餓了。

例 But you just ate.
但你剛吃過了啊。

⑦
吃飯

我們去吃點東西

Let's go grab a bite.

解析

在這裡使用的是比較常會出現在日常生活的對話，除了說Let's eat something. 最常用的就是這句了。

會話 1

例 Let's go grab a bite!

我們去吃點東西吧！

例 Good idea.

好主意。

會話 2

例 We should go grab a bite.

我們應該去吃點東西。

例 But I am still busy here.

可是我還沒有忙完。

🎧 track 103

你想去哪吃？
What do you propose?

解析

不知道該去哪兒吃或是該吃些什麼時，問對方有沒有什麼好提議就可以這樣說囉！

會話 1

例 I'm starving.

我好餓哦。

例 Me too. What do you propose?

我也是，你有想要去哪吃嗎？

會話 2

例 I want to take my girlfriend to a nice restaurant. What do you propose?

我想帶我女朋友去很不錯的地方吃飯，你有什麼提議嗎？

例 What kind of food does she like?

她喜歡怎麼樣的菜？

7
吃飯

我現在沒有很餓
I don't feel hungry now.

解析

若是有人邀約吃東西，但是自己不是很餓的時候就可以這樣說，或者是想拒絕邀約時也可以這麼說啦。

會話 1

例 We are going to eat pizza. Do you want to come?

我們要去吃披薩，你要來嗎？

例 No, thanks. I don't feel hungry now.

不了，謝謝，我現在不餓。

會話 2

例 Let's go grab a bite.

我們去吃點東西吧！

例 But I don't feel hungry now.

可是我現在沒有很餓。

🎧track 104

想吃點什麼

What would you like to eat?

解 析

這是很常用的問對方想吃什麼，或是在點餐的時候通常都會尋問朋友的意見，這時候都是用這句話來表示。

會話1

例 What would you like to eat?
你想吃什麼？

例 BBQ!
烤肉！

會話2

例 What would you like to eat?
想吃點什麼？

例 I would like to have a piece of chocolate cakc.
我想要一塊巧克力蛋糕。

我要和朋友吃飯

I will meet my friends for dinner.

解析

不管是晚餐還是午餐，跟什麼人見面，都能夠運用自如，只需替換幾個關鍵字就可以了哦！

會話 1

例 What is your plan tonight?
你今晚要幹嘛？

例 I will meet my friends for dinner.
我要和朋友吃飯。

會話 2

例 It is so early. Where are you going?
還很早耶，你要去哪裡？

例 I am going to meet my classmates for breakfast.
我要去跟我同學吃早餐。

我要和家人吃飯

I will have lunch/dinner with my family.

解析

家人的事總是第一優先，所以當有人約，又不巧的那天要與家人相聚，就可以這樣說囉。

會話1

例 We will have a pool party tonight. I wish you could come.

今晚有游池派對，希望你能來。

例 I'm sorry, I will have dinner with my family.

抱歉，我要和家人吃飯。

會話2

例 I will have lunch with my family, maybe next time.

我要和家人吃飯，下次吧。

❼吃飯

例 Sure, I will call you.

沒問題，我再打給你。

我和男/女朋友要約會

I have a date.

解 析

有約會要出去吃飯，可是又不是男女朋友的關係，該怎麼說呢？就簡單的說有一個 date 就可以了。

會話 1

例 Do you want to go to the movie with us tonight?

你今天晚上要跟我們去看電影嗎？

例 I can't. I have a date.

不行，我有一個約會。

會話 2

例 Hey, who is the girl I saw last time, your girlfriend?

嘿，我上次看到的那個女生是你女朋友嗎？

例 No, she is a date.

不是，只是一個約會的對象。

🎧 track 106

我想訂位

I want to make a reservation.

解析

非常重要的訂位話術，只要是去餐廳訂位就是這樣說啦！所以千萬要牢牢記住。或是有時候會說「我要一張桌子」，沒錯，可以用 May I have a table for five? 我可以要一張五個人的桌子嗎？

會話 1

例 Hi, this is TGI Friday, may I help you?

嗨，這裡是星期五餐廳，請問需要什麼呢？

例 I want to make a reservation for 5 people.

我要訂五個人的位子。

會話 2

例 Do you have a reservation?

你們有訂位嗎？

例 Yes. Mr. Chen, six people.

有的，陳先生，六位。

我要確認訂位

I want to confirm the reservation.

解析

不管是餐廳打來確認，還是是因為人數有更動而告知餐廳，confirm 和 double-check 都是有確認和再次核對的意思哦。

會話 1

例 Hi, this is Mary's Pizza. We would like to confirm the reservation for 5 people at 8 o'clock tonight.

嗨，這裡是瑪莉披薩店，想跟您確認今晚是八點五位的訂位。

例 Yes, exactly.

是的,沒錯。

會話 2

例 Hi, I would like to double-check my reservation.

你好,我想再次確認我的訂位。

例 Sure, may I have your last name and phone number?

沒問題,可以給我你的姓和電話號碼嗎?

track 107

點飲料

We want to order something to drink.

解析

通常在餐廳點餐,決定餐點的時間會比較久,這時候除了服務生會問你要不要先點飲料,自己也可以先請服務生上飲料來解解渴再慢慢看要吃什麼。

7 吃飯

會話 1

例 Can I get you something to drink first?
你們要不要先點飲料呢？

例 Yeah, one fresh orange juice and one beer, please.
好啊，一個新鮮柳橙汁和一個啤酒，謝謝。

會話 2

例 We want to order some drinks.
我們想要點飲料。

例 Sure.
沒問題。

餐前/隨餐/餐後上

Come before/with/after the meal.

解析

點完飲料後，通常會被問到請問是要餐前上，隨餐上，還是餐後再上，就依個人喜好來決定囉。

會話 1

例 I want my beer served with the meal, thanks.

我的啤酒要隨餐上。

例 No problem.

好的。

會話 2

例 Would you like your coffee to come after the meal?

您想要咖啡最後上嗎?

例 Yes, please.

沒錯,謝謝。

track 108

可以點餐了

We are ready to order.

⑦ 吃飯

解 析

當準備好要點餐時該怎麼說呢?I want to order. 雖然沒有錯,但是卻不是一句大家

會用的話，所以這裡就是教大家講「準備好可以點餐了」。

會話 1

例 Are you ready to order?

準備好點餐了嗎？

例 We haven't decided yet, can we have five more minutes?

我們還沒決定，可以再五分鐘嗎？

會話 2

例 Excuse me. We are ready to order.

不好意思，我們可以點餐了。

例 Just a second.

我馬上來。

可以看一下菜單嗎？

Can I have the menu, please?

解析

不管是菜單還是酒單還是飲料單，都可以稱它為menu，有時候酒單會說是 wine list，但只要是有需要就可以這麼說。

會話1

例 Can I help you?

需要什麼嗎？

例 Can I have two more menus, please?

可以再給我兩本菜單嗎？

會話2

例 Do you need the wine list?

您需要看酒單嗎？

例 No, thanks.

不用了謝謝。

track 109

我吃太飽了

I'm full.

解析

吃的太飽了！這句頻繁使用的句子該怎麼說呢？除了說 I ate too much. 我吃太多了之外，用 I'm full.用來貼切形容，我肚子被塞的滿滿的。

迷你短句

會話 1

例 What would you like for dessert?
你甜點想要吃什麼？

例 I'm too full. I don't want dessert.
我太飽了，我不想要吃甜點了。

會話 2

例 I'm full. What about you?
我吃好飽哦，你呢？

例 I feel nothing. I'm still hungry.
我沒有感覺，還是好餓哦。

吃不完外帶

I want take out / it to go

解析

除了課本都會教的For here or to go? 這裡用還是外帶？這裡也順便講一下吃不完要打包怎麼辦呢？這時候這句話就派的上用場了。

會話 1

例 I'm so full.
我好飽哦。

例 You can take it to go.
吃不完可以外帶。

會話 2

例 Are you sure you have enough time to eat here?
你確定你有時間在這邊吃嗎？

例 You think we should get take out?
你認為我們應該外帶哦？

🎧track 110

不滿意服務

I did not pay for this.

解析

若是遇到出去買東西或是餐廳用餐，不滿意所得到的服務時，總是會很氣憤，這時會怎麼說呢？就會說：我花錢不是為了得到這樣的東西！

⑦ 吃飯

會話 1

例 What the heck is this?

這是什麼鬼東西？

例 We are very sorry. We will give you a new one.

我們非常抱歉，會再重做一份新的給您。

例 I did not pay for this!

我花錢是來吃這個的嗎？

會話 2

例 I did not pay for this!

這不是我付錢想得到的服務！

例 Take it easy.

放輕鬆一點。

我要跟你們經理談談

I need to talk to your manager.

解析

不滿意服務到了要客訴的時候怎麼辦！中文常常說：叫你們經理出來！其實英文也

差不多，就是請一個能作主的人出來表示誠意囉！

會話 1

例 Can I talk to someone in charge?
我可以和這裡負責的人談談嗎？

例 That will be me.
我就是。

會話 2

例 I need to talk to your manager.
我要找你們經理談。

例 The manager is not here today.
今天經理不在。

🎧track 111

滿意服務

We enjoyed your service.

解析

其實也不用講這麼長的一段話，也是可以表示對服務滿意，譬如說 good service! 也是可以的。

⑦ 吃飯

會話 1

例 We really enjoyed your service.
我們很滿意你們的服務。

例 It is our pleasure.
是我們的榮幸。

會話 2

例 How did you like the restaurant?
你喜歡這家餐廳的什麼地方？

例 They have really good service.
他們服務很好。

結帳

Check. / Can I get the bill?

解析

買單！該怎麼說呢？在一個語言不同的國家可能用手勢比一下就好了，但是可以用英語溝通的地方當然要把所學給展現出來，用 Check, please. 或是 Can I get the bill. 都可以。

會話1

例 Check, please.
　買單。

例 It's $890.
　一共是八百九十元。

會話2

例 Can I get the bill?
　我要買單。

例 Here, sir. By the way, we don't take credit cards.
　這是您的帳單，順便跟您說我們不收信用卡。

 ⌂track 112

慢用！
Enjoy!

❼
吃飯

解析

開動囉！請慢用，享受你的食物該怎麼說呢？簡單的用 Enjoy! 就可以囉！

會話 1

例 Enjoy your salad.
請享用你的沙拉。

例 Thank you.
謝謝你。

會話 2

例 Yay! My steak!
耶！我的牛排來了！

例 Enjoy!
好好享用吧！

選的好！

Good choice

解 析

點東西吃的時候，如果別人點的東西看起來好像很棒，通常就會說：看起來不錯哦！選的好！

會話 1

例 What would you like?
你想要吃什麼？

例 Aunt Grey's special breakfast.

葛蕾阿姨特製早餐。

例 Good choice!

選的好！

會話2

例 I would like a blueberry bagel and cream cheese.

我要一個藍莓貝果加乳酪。

例 That's a good choice.

好選擇。

track 113

有推薦的嗎？

Any recommendations?

解析

餐單看來看去都不知道該點什麼才好，這時候就會問旁邊的人或是服務生，有沒有特別推薦的啊？也可以說 What do you suggest? 你有建議的嗎？

會話 1

例 Ready to order?
準備好點餐了嗎？

例 Not really. Any recommendations?
還沒。有任何推薦的嗎？

會話 2

例 What do you suggest?
你有建議的嗎？

例 I know their chicken is good.
我知道他們的雞肉很不錯。

今日特餐是什麼？

What's today's special?

解析

一般來説到餐廳吃飯，當天一定都有所謂的今日特餐，通常就是指當天才有的食材或是有特別活動的餐點，不妨問一下囉！

會話 1

例 Are you ready to order?
要點餐了嗎？

例 What's today's special?

今日特餐是什麼？

會話 2

例 Does today's special include salad?

今日特餐有包括沙拉嗎？

例 No, it doesn't.

沒有。

🎧 track 114

請用

Here you are.

解 析

上菜或是在遞東西的時候，遞到他人面前就是用 Here you are. 或是 Here you go. 通常就是「請」、「拿去」的意思。

會話 1

例 Here you are, cheese burger and bagel.

請用，這是您的起司漢堡和貝果。

例 Thank you.

謝謝。

會話 2

例 How much?

多少錢？

例 It's NT$250.

一共二百五十元。

例 Here is NT$300.

這裡是三百元。

例 Here you go, NT$50 change.

五十元零錢找您。

要熱一點

I want it extra hot.

解 析

有時候點飲料還是食物都覺得好像很快就涼掉了，更別說是要外帶到遠一點的地方，如果這時需要熱一點，就可以這麼說囉。

會話 1

例 Can I have my soup extra hot?

我的湯可以熱一點嗎？

例 Yes, of course.
　好的，當然可以。

會話 2

例 What would you like to have?
　您想要點什麼呢？

例 A large latte.
　大杯拿鐵。

例 Iced or hot?
　冰的還是熱的？

例 Hot, extra hot.
　熱的，要熱一點。

🎧 track 115

他食物中毒
He got food poisoning.

7
吃飯

解析

　食物中毒就是 food poisoning，是名詞哦，當有人食物中毒的時候，這樣說就對了。

會話 1

例 He got food poisoning.

他食物中毒。

例 What about you? Did you eat the same thing?

那你呢？你們有吃一樣的東西嗎？

會話 2

例 I don't feel well. I guess it was the clams.

我不太舒服，我想是因為蛤蜊。

例 You got food poisoning!

你食物中毒了！

我可以續杯嗎？

Can I get a refill?

解析

最好用的句子！續杯！get another one? 不不不，有專門的字來表示續杯哦！那就是 refill，再裝滿的意思。

會話 1

例 I need a refill.
我需要續杯。

例 Ok, no problem.
好的,沒問題。

會話 2

例 Can I refill my coffee?
我的咖啡可以續杯嗎?

例 Of course.
當然。

🎧 track 116

幫我把…拿掉

Can you please take out the....

解析

每個人都有自己不喜歡吃或是不能吃的東西,通常在點餐時都會請餐廳把某樣東西拿掉,甚至在速食店也可以這樣,那該怎麼説呢?

會話 1

例 I would like a cheese burger.

我要一個起司漢堡。

例 Ok.

好的。

例 Can you take out the tomato?

可以把蕃茄拿掉嗎？

會話 2

例 How can you take out the cheese if you order a cheese burger?

你怎麼可以點了起司漢堡又要把起司拿掉？

例 Why can't I?

為什麼不行？

我對…過敏

I am allergic to ….

解析

對特定食物過敏的人，出去外面吃飯一定會很小心，都會先問菜裡有沒有什麼會讓

自己過敏的東西，這時就可以說：我對…
過敏。

會話 1

例 Are you allergic to peanuts?

你對花生過敏嗎？

例 No, I just don't like them.

沒有啊，我只是不喜歡而已。

會話 2

例 You are breaking out in a rash!

你長了好多疹子哦！

例 Oh! Must be the soup! I am allergic
to shrimp!

哦！一定是湯！我對蝦子過敏！

 🎧 track 117

需要糖或奶精嗎？

Do you need any sugar or cream?

7
吃飯

解 析

喝咖啡或是喝茶的時候，都會問別人需要
糖和奶精嗎？可以記下來加以運用哦！

會話 1

例 Do you need any sugar or cream in your coffee?

你的咖啡需要糖或奶精嗎?

例 No, I like it black.

不用,我喜歡黑咖啡。

會話 2

例 Do you have milk?

你們有牛奶嗎?

例 I'm sorry. We don't.

很抱歉我們沒有。

你的主菜想要吃什麼?

What would you like for your main course?

解析

也可以問前菜 appetizer、點心 dessert 或是飲料 drink。

會話1

例 What would you like for your main course?

請問你的主菜想要點什麼呢？

例 Any suggestions?

有推薦嗎？

例 You can try our mutton chops.

你可以試試我們的羊小排。

會話2

例 What would you likc for your appetizer?

你的前菜想要吃什麼？

例 Smoked salmon. Can you take out the onions?

燻鮭魚，可以不要放洋蔥嗎？

 ∩track 118

我牛排想要…分熟

I would like it rare / medium / well-done.

解析

問牛排要幾分熟，就是 How would you like your steak? 回答其實除了從 rare 到 well-done 中間還是可以分更細的，rare, medium rare, medium, medium well, well-done.

會話 1

例 How would you like your steak?
你的牛排要幾分熟？

例 Medium rare, thank you.
稍熟，謝謝。

會話 2

例 I can't eat my steak very rare.
我不能吃完全生的牛肉。

例 Why? I think it is tasty.
為什麼？我覺得很好吃啊。

例 It feels like eating my own flesh.
感覺好像在吃自己的肉。

你需要多吃一些蔬菜

You should eat more vegetables.

解 析

多吃蔬菜水果對身體好，要怎麼樣對那些肉食者說呢？eat more 就對了！

會 話

例 Can I change my side dish?

我可以換我的小菜嗎？

例 Sure.

可以。

例 I want to change broccoli to French fries.

我想要把花椰菜換成薯條。

例 You should eat more vegetables.

你應該要多吃一些蔬菜。

track 119

你應該少吃一點速食

You should eat less fast food.

解析

速食又方便又好吃，讓人很難抗拒，可是太常吃卻有可能對身體造成負擔哦！所以要勸人少吃一點就可以這麼說囉

會話 1

例 Your son eats too much fast food.
你的兒子吃太多速食了。

例 But he really likes it.
但是他真的很喜歡。

會話 2

例 You should eat less fast food.
你應該少吃一點速食。

例 I know. I am getting fat.
我知道，我越來越肥胖了。

我們應該吃健康一點
We should eat healthier.

解 析

想要吃健康一點該怎麼説呢？有好多有機的食物和蔬果都是吃健康一點的好選擇哦。

會話 1

例 We should eat healthier.
我們應該吃健康一點。

例 How?
怎麼做？

例 Start by eating less fast food.
從少吃一點速食開始。

會話 2

例 Only eating vegetables will not make you thinner.
只有吃那些蔬果不會讓你變瘦。

例 I know. I am exercising too.
我知道，我也有在運動啦。

🎧 track 120

你要給小費

You need to tip.

解析

雖然在台灣沒有給小費的習慣，可是在國外很多地方還是都需要給小費的，這時候該怎麼説呢？

會話 1

例 Do we need to tip here?
這裡需要給小費嗎？

例 Yes, I think we do.
我覺得我們應該要給小費。

會話 2

例 Those rich people never tip.
那些有錢人從不給小費。

例 They always think the service is not good enough.
他們都認為服務不夠好啊。

你們有素食嗎？

Do you have vegetarian dishes?

解析

跟吃素的人一起用餐一定要為對方先著想
才是，雖然他們是少數，但是挑選餐廳的
時候就要先問一下囉。

會話1

例 Do you have any vegetarian dishes?
你們有供應素食嗎？

例 No, we don't.
沒有。

會話2

例 Are you a vegetarian?
你是素食者嗎？

例 No. I just don't like to eat meat.
不是，我只是不愛吃肉。

我不怎麼愛喝咖啡

I'm not keen on coffee.

解析

Keen是有熱衷、強烈渴望的意思，其實後面放的名詞可以是任何東西，用來表示自己可以接受這個東西，但並不是太喜歡。

會話 1

例 Would you like some coffee, ma'am?

女士，請問要來點咖啡嗎？

例 Tea will be fine. I'm not keen on coffee.

茶就可以了，我不怎麼愛喝咖啡。

會話 2

例 Rice or noodles

吃飯還是麵？

例 Noodles maybe? I'm not keen on rice.

麵吧？我不怎麼愛吃飯。

MORNING ROUTINE

 LEMON WATER

 FITNESS

 SHOWER

 BEAUTY ROUTINE

 BREAKFAST

Chapter

8

娛樂

最近有什麼好看的電影
Do you know of any good movies recently?

解析

想要看電影又不知道有什麼電影好看，這時可能就會問身旁的朋友，最近有什麼好看的電影啊？

會話 1

例 Do you know of any good movies recently?

最近有什麼好看的電影啊？

例 Batman?

蝙蝠俠？

會話 2

例 Do you know of any good movies recently?

最近有什麼好看的電影啊？

例 I don't know. You should Google it.

不知道耶，你去查一下。

你想跟我去看電影嗎
Can I take you to a movie?

解析

通常這樣講take someone to意思是你會請客，如果不是想要請對方一起去的話，就說Do you want to see a movie? 就可以了。

會話1

例 Can I take you to a movie?
你想跟我去看電影嗎？

例 Is this a date?
是約會嗎？

會話2

例 You should take me to a movie.
你應該要帶我去看電影。

例 Why?
為什麼？

例 Because it is my birthday.
因為是我生日啊。

○track 122

你想怎麼買票？

How do you want to get the tickets?

解析

現在不管是什麼票，都有很多種方式可以買，譬如說網路上、便利商店或是現場買等等，這時候就會問要一起去的朋友，比較想要用什麼方式買票才方便呢？

會話 1

例 How do you want to get the tickets?

你想怎麼買票？

例 I can get them at 7-11.

我可以去 7-11 買。

會話 2

例 I think it will be cheaper to get the tickets online.

好像網路上買票比較便宜。

例 No, it won't. You just don't need to get in a long line.

不會，只是你就不需要排隊而已。

是幾點開始？
What time is the movie/show?

解析

這句重要的話當然要學起來啦，不然遲到或是早到都糗大，所以不管是去看電影還是表演都要問清楚是幾點開始。

會話 1

例 What time is the movie?
電影幾點開始？
7:30.
七點半。

會話 2

例 Do you know what time the show is?
你知道表演是幾點開始嗎？

例 I am not sure. I'll have to check again.
我不太確定，我要再查一下。

退票、退回

I need a refund.

解析

買了票有時候總是會遇到突發狀況，遇到
需要退票時該怎麼說呢？就是用refund來
表示囉。用在其它地方，就是有退錢、退
貨的意思。

會話 1

例 I bought the wrong tickets. I messed
up the dates.

我買錯票了，我搞錯日期。

例 Then we need to get a refund.

那我們要去退票。

會話 2

例 I need a refund. This is not the size
I want.

我要退錢，這個不是我想要的尺寸。

例 Sure, can I see your reccipt?

好的，我可以看一下你的收據嗎？

8
娛樂

不能退的
It is not refundable.

解 析

曉得退回該怎麼說了，那時候萬一是不能
夠退的東西怎麼辦？對方會說：這是不能
退的，那自己聽到這句話就要知道是什麼
意思囉。

會 話 1

例 Can I get a refund for this?
請問這個可以退嗎？

例 Sorry, this is not refundable.
抱歉，這是不能退的。

會 話 2

例 All the merchandise with yellow tags
are not refundable.
所有黃標商品都不能退貨。

例 Ok, thank you.
好的，謝謝。

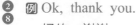

🎧track 124

可以換位子嗎？
Can I change my seat?

解析

去看表演或是電影時，萬一不滿意自己的位子怎麼辦呢？想換位子的時候就要知道該怎麼說。

會話1

例 I can't see clearly. The guy in front of me is too tall.

我看不清楚，我前面那個人太高了。

例 Do you want to change your seat?

你想要換位子嗎？

會話2

例 Can I change my seat with you? I want to sit with my friend.

我可以跟你換位子嗎？我想跟我朋友坐。

例 Yeah, sure.

哦好啊。

8
娛樂

可以拍照嗎？
Can I take photos here?

解析

去看很多展覽或是表演的時候不一定都可以拍照，所以如果不清楚的話就可以先問一下囉。

會話1

例 Excuse me? Can I take photos here?
不好意思，這裡可以拍照嗎？

例 Yes, you can, but no flash.
可以，但是不能用閃光。

會話2

例 Excuse me. You can't take photos here.
不好意思，這裡不能拍照。

例 Oh, sorry.
哦，抱歉。

我忘記帶証件

I forgot my ID.

解 析

有時候出去玩必須確認身份或是年紀，這時就需要出示任何有效證明啦，萬一剛好忘記帶了怎麼辦！那就只好這麼說囉。

會 話 1

例 Can I see your ID, please?

我可以看一下你的身份證嗎？

例 Oh, no. I forgot my ID.

噢，不好了，我忘記帶證件了。

會 話 2

例 How old are you? You can't enter if you're under 20.

你幾歲啊？20歲以下不能進去哦。

例 It will be fine. I look old.

沒事的，我看起來很老啊。

例 They will check your ID.

他們會檢查你的證件的。

8
娛樂

她/他真是太過氣了

S / he is all washed-up.

解 析

這句話感覺有點不禮貌，但是有時候要去看某位資深明星演的電影或是演唱會，如果不是自己喜歡的，就會跟朋友説：那個人真是有點過氣了。

會 話

例 We are going to watch that action movie tomorrow.

我們明天要去看那部動作片。

例 Really? Don't you think he is all washed-up?

真的嗎？你們不覺得他很過氣嗎？

例 The hot girl is the reason, not him.

辣妹才是我們去看的理由，又不是他。

例 But I still think he is too old to be in that kind of film.

但我還是覺得演這種電影他太老了。

如你所願囉
As you wish.

解析

這句話的意思就是：好的。答應別人什麼
事的時候，就好像在幫別人完成願望一
樣，所以就會用 As you wish. 來表示好的
意思。

會話1

例 Can we have dinner at the French restaurant that I've always wanted to go to?

我們可以去那間我一直很想去的法國餐廳
吃晚餐嗎？

例 As you wish.

如你所願囉。

會話2

例 Dinner or movie?

看電影還是吃晚餐？

例 Both

都要。

8
娛樂

例 As you wish.

好的。

希望不會冒犯你

Hope it is not offensive.

解析

其實先講了這句之後，好像就是為了後面要講的話先上了一層潤滑劑一樣，就好像先說：我希望我沒有打擾到你，請問你可以幫我一個忙嗎？是很像的道理。

會話 1

例 Hope it is not offensive.

希望不會冒犯到你。

例 What is it?

是什麼事？

例 I think you look more beautiful with dark hair.

我覺得你染深色頭髮比較漂亮。

會話 2

例 I don't like this advertisement. It materializes the female.

我不喜歡這個廣告，它物化女性。

例 Yeah, I feel offended.

沒錯，我覺得很反感。

🎧 track 127

她/他一定會嚇一跳

S/he will freak out.

解析

Freak out 可以用作嚇一跳、嚇壞了或是
抓狂，如果是抓狂的話，也可以說 drive
someone crazy/nuts

會話 1

例 Look at the fake cockroach I just
bought!

看我剛買的假蟑螂！

例 Don't let Rita scc it, she will freak out.

不要讓麗塔看到，她會嚇壞的。

會話 2

例 Let's go watch that horror movie!

我們去看那部恐怖片吧！

例 Seriously? I will be freaking out.

認真的嗎？我一定會嚇破膽。

太好了/太棒了/太可笑了

That is wonderful / terrific / ridiculous!

解析

驚呼用語，看到什麼超棒的東西、超爛的東西，都可以這麼說，把形容詞換掉就可以囉。

會話 1

例 What do you think about the concert?

你覺得演唱會怎麼樣？

例 That was wonderful!

真是太棒了！

會話 2

例 Can you believe that we met David Beckham?

你能相信剛剛我們遇到大衛貝克漢嗎？

例 That was unbelievable!

那真的是令人不置信！

track 128

太可惜了/太遺憾了

That is too bad.

解析

這句話很好用的地方是，聽到人家說什麼不好的事，如果要回應又不知道要說些什麼的時候，就可以說：哦真是太可惜了！真是太遺憾了！

會話 **1**

例 I did not get the tickets to the show.

我沒有買到票。

例 That is too bad.

太可惜了。

會話 **2**

例 I don't feel well. I'm afraid I can't go to the party with you.

我不太舒服，我可能不能跟你們去派對了。

例 All right. That's too bad.

好吧，太可惜了。

這恐怕不在行程裡

It is not on the wish list.

解析

不在原本的計畫或是要表示不在考慮的範圍內該怎麼說呢？願望清單wish list就可以這樣表示。

會話1

例 Maybe we can drop by the ice cream house.

也許我們可以順道在冰淇淋屋那邊停一下。

例 I'm afraid it is not on the wish list.

我想這恐怕不在行程裡哦。

會話2

例 This is my wish list of what I want on my birthday.

這是我生日想要的願望清單。

例 Dear, I'm afraid getting a dog can't be on the list.

親愛的，恐怕養狗沒辦法放在清單裡哦。

 ○track 129

我別無選擇了

I don't have a choice.

解析

感覺好像是被逼到絕境的時候會說的話：我沒有其它選擇了！表示真的是沒有辦法了。

會話 1

例 So we have decided to go to the Italian restaurant.

所以我們已經決定了要去義大利餐廳了。

例 Looks like I don't have a choice.

看來我也沒有其它選擇了。

會話 2

例 Our seats sucked.

我們的座位好爛。

迷你短句

例 We were late, so we didn't have other choices, ok?

我們太晚到了，沒有什麼其它的選擇了好嗎？

你需要運動了

You need to exercise.

解析

適當的運動是好事，需要提醒親朋好友爸爸媽媽兄弟姐妹記得要運動！

會話 1

例 You need to exercise.

你需要運動了。

例 I feel fine.

我感覺很好啊。

會話 2

例 I think I need to exercise.

我想我需要運動一下。

例 You can go swimming with me.

你可以跟我去游泳。

🎧track 130

我們去逛街
Let's go shopping.

解析

逛街是一件很美妙的事啊，無聊的時候找
找好朋友或是家人一起去逛街該怎麼說
呢？

會話 1

例 Let's go shopping!
我們去逛街吧！

例 I can't. I don't have money.
我不行，我沒錢了。

會話 2

例 Let's go shopping or go to a movie!
我們去逛街或是看電影！

例 Why are you always spending money?
你為什麼總是在花錢啊？

有一間新開的店

There is a new store that opened.

解析

有新開的店要找朋友去嚐鮮，有可能是服飾店、餐廳、酒吧等等的，就可以邀請對方跟自己一同前往看看囉。

會話 1

例 There is a new bar that opened. Do you want to go this weekend?

有一間新開的酒吧，你這個週末想去嗎？

例 Yeah, sure.

好啊。

會話 2

例 There is a new accessory store that opened; do you want to take a look?

有一間新開的飾品店，你想去逛逛嗎？

例 I've already been there. It was not really exciting.

我去過了，其實東西還好。

track 131

你喜歡做什麼運動？

What kind of sports do you like?

解析

其實運動也是一個不錯的話題，不但可以找到同好又有益健康，想問對方喜歡什麼樣的運動時就可以這麼說囉！

會話1

例 What kind of sports do you like?
你喜歡什麼樣的運動呢？

例 I like swimming.
我喜歡游泳。

例 Me too!
我也是耶。

會話 2

例 What kind of sports do you like?

你喜歡什麼樣的運動呢？

例 I was a basketball team player in high school.

我高中是籃球校隊。

例 Impressive!

太厲害了。

我喜歡打網球(球類運動)
I like to play tennis.

解析

球類運動該怎麼說呢？桌球：table tennis
籃球：basketball棒球：baseball壘球：
softball排球：volleyball美式足球：football
英式足球：soccer羽毛球：badminton英式
橄欖球：rugby壁球：squash保齡球：
bowling曲棍球：hokey高爾夫：golf

會話 1

例 Do you play basketball?

你打籃球嗎？

例 No, I don't. But I play soccer.

我不打籃球，可是我踢足球。

會話 2

例 What's your favorite ball game?

你最喜歡的球類運動是什麼？

例 Rugby!

英式橄欖球！

 🎧 track 132

我喜歡騎腳踏車
I like biking.

解析

最近騎腳踏車已成為一個新運動趨勢，所以如果自己的運動是騎車，就可以這樣說囉。

會話 1

例 Do you like biking?

你喜歡騎腳踏車嗎？

例 Yes, I do. I go biking every weekend.

喜歡啊，我每個週末都去騎車。

會話 2

例 I like your mountain bike!

我喜歡你的山地車！

例 Thanks! This is my brother's. That road bike is mine.

謝啦，這是我哥哥的，那台公路車才是我的。

我喜歡跳舞

I like dancing.

解析

舞蹈也有很多種類，譬如說芭蕾：ballet 爵士：jazz 嘻哈街舞：hip-hop 踢踏舞：tap 肚皮舞：belly dance 現代舞：modern dance 國際標準舞：ballroom dance 等等的。跳舞也是很不錯的運動呢。

會話 1

例 Do you dance?

你跳舞嗎？

例 Not really. I just move my toes most of the time.

不盡然，我都只是動動腳趾而已。

會話 2

例 I like dancing.

我喜歡跳舞。

例 What kind of dance do you do?

你都跳什麼舞？

例 I am a hip-hop dancer.

我是街舞舞者。

 track 133

我想呼吸新鮮空氣
I need some fresh air.

解 析

閊在室內悶壞了該出去透透氣該怎麼説呢？這時候就可以説：我想要呼吸一些新鮮空氣！

會 話 1

例 I don't like smoke.

我不喜歡煙味。

例 Do you need some fresh air?

你需要透透氣嗎？

會 話 2

例 I need some fresh air.

我需要呼吸新鮮空氣。

例 Sure. I'll go with you.

好的，我陪你。

我想去旅行

I want to go traveling.

解 析

若是需要休息、想要放鬆一下，到自己喜歡的地方旅行該怎麼表示呢？就可以説：

I want to go traveling. 或是I want to go
for a trip.

會話 1

例 I want to go traveling.
我想要去旅行。

例 Where would you like to go?
你想去哪裡。

例 Anywhere but here.
只要離開這裡就好。

會話 2

例 I don't want to go to the South.
我不想要去南部。

例 It is a family trip!
這可是家庭旅遊！

 track 134

我想去聽演唱會
I want to go to the concert.

解析

演唱會總是一個令人興奮的事件，可以享受音樂又可以見到喜愛的歌手，當然也要邀朋友一同共襄盛舉了！

會話1

例 Have you heard that Maroon 5 is coming?

你有聽說魔力紅要來開演唱會嗎？

例 Of course! I am definitely going.

當然，我一定要去的啊。

會話2

例 I want to go to the concert.

我想要去看演唱會。

例 But I heard she couldn't sing well live.

但是我聽說她唱現場不好聽。

票太貴了

I cannot afford the ticket.

解 析

演唱會雖然很吸引人，可是大部份視野比較好的票都很貴，尤其是國外的藝人來更是貴翻天，這時候就算想去也是力不從心啊。

會話 **1**

例 I really want to go to the concert, but I cannot afford the ticket.

我真的好想去看演唱會哦，可是票太貴了。

例 I can't afford it, either.

我也買不起。

會話 **2**

例 Do you want to see Lady Gaga?

你要去看卡卡的演唱會嗎？

例 I'd love to, but I can't afford the ticket. The price is freaking me out.

我很想但是我買不起票，那個價格真是嚇死我了。

◯ track 135

你可以參加抽獎活動

You can join the lucky draw.

解析

常常講到抽獎抽獎，那到底應該怎麼說呢？就是Lucky draw!

會話 1

例 You can save your ticket stub for the lucky draw.

你可以把票根留下來參加抽獎。

例 Cool.

好棒哦。

會話 2

例 You can join the lucky draw.

你可以參加抽獎活動。

例 Yeah, maybe I will get a car.

是啊，也許我會抽到一台車。

我想去海邊！
I want to go to the beach!

解析

炎炎夏日，到海邊玩是大部份人一定會做的事，那英文該怎麼說，簡簡單單的說就是 I want to go to the beach! 順便說一下衝浪就是：surfing

會話 1

例 I want to go to the beach.
我想要去海邊。

例 It's a perfect day to go.
今天最適合去海邊了。

會話 2

例 I want to go surfing.
我想去衝浪。

例 I know a great beach for surfing.
我知道有一個很棒的海灘可以衝浪哦。

track 136

你知道音樂節嗎？

Do you know about the music festival?

解析

音樂節就是連續好幾天不休息的音樂盛會，有很多不同的主題，有電子音樂、搖滾樂團，或是流行音樂等等，通常一次就是二、三天，讓大家一同享受音樂。

會話 1

例 Do you know about the music festival next week?

你知道下禮拜有音樂節嗎？

例 Of course, that is the biggest event of the year!

當然啊，那可是一年最大的盛事耶！

會話 2

例 How was the music festival?

那個音樂季怎麼樣？

例 It was terrific!

實在是太棒了！

夕陽真的超美的

The sunset is amazing.

解析

不管是去海邊還是山上，總是有可能會看
到難得的夕陽或日出，令人嘆為觀止的夕
陽該怎麼説呢？

會話1

例 It is too bad that you didn't go with us.

你沒有跟我們去真的太可惜了。

例 How was it?

好玩嗎？

例 The sunset is amazing!

夕陽真的是太美了！

會話2

例 We might see the sunrise if we are
lucky.

如果幸運的話我們也許能看到日出哦。

8
娛樂

迷你短句

例 I don't think I can get up so early.

我覺得我爬不起來。

🎧 track 137

那裡的食物很有特色

The food there is very exotic.

解析

exotic是形容很有異國風情的味道,如果
是品嚐一些特殊當地的食物,就可以這麼
說囉。

會話 **1**

例 How was the food in Dubai?

杜拜那裡的食物怎麼樣?

例 Some of it was very exotic.

有些還滿有特色的。

會話 **2**

例 I want to try some exotic food, not
always rice and noodles.

我想要試一些很有異國風情的食物,不要
一直都吃飯和麵。

例 Let me see what I can do.

讓我想看看。

文化差異

It is a cultural difference.

解析

去到一個不同的國家或是和不同文化的人相處，一定會有不一樣的磨擦，也許等是彼此是的觀念、價值觀等等，這時候就會說是文化差異。

會話 1

例 Do you and your boyfriend have any cultural differences?

你和你男朋友會有文化上的差異嗎？

例 A little. But we would try to work it out.

有一點吧，但是我們都會試著去解決。

會話 2

例 You can't look down on them just because they eat with their hands.

你不可以因為他們用手吃飯就看不起他們。

例 I don't! It is just a cultural difference, and I just feel weird.

我沒有啊！我知道是文化差異，但我只是覺得很奇怪嘛。

🎧 track 138

現在不是去那個地方的好時機
It is not the best time to visit.

解析

什麼時候會用到這句話咧？可能是某些地方有動亂、災害、氣候等等因素，就會跟對方說，現在可能不是去某些地方旅遊的好時機哦！

會話 1

例 What do you think if we go to Japan?

你覺得我們去日本怎麼樣？

例 Maybe it is not the best time to visit after the earthquake.

在地震過後現在去似乎不是個好時機。

會話 2

例 Where did you go last weekend?

你上個週末去哪玩啊？

例 I went to Green Island, and it was not that good.

我去綠島但不怎麼好玩。

例 Yeah, it was not the best time to visit during a typhoon.

是啊，颱風來的時候應該不是個好時機去玩。

我是伴娘

I am a bridesmaid.

解 析

其實重點就是 bridesmaid 伴娘這個字，結婚時大家都只知道新娘是 bride，但是伴娘的身份也很重要，所以現在就知道囉。

會話 1

例 Can I be a bridesmaid?

我可以當伴娘嗎？

例 Are you single?

你還是單身嗎？

會話 2

例 Who is the bridesmaid?

那個伴娘是誰啊？

例 She is the bride's best friend.

她是新娘最好的朋友。

 track 139

我是伴郎

I am the best man.

解析

新郎是 groom，那伴郎就是 best man 啦！
除了主角知道怎麼說之外，配角也很重要
哦！

會話 1

例 I am the best man.

我是伴郎。

例 What is your plan for the bachelor party?

那你的單身派對要怎麼計劃？

會話 2

例 Being the best man is really not easy.

當伴郎很不容易耶。

例 I know. You have to take care of a lot of things.

我知道啊，你必須照料很多事。

那是我最愛的作家

That is my favorite writer.

解析

娛樂當然也包括了看展覽、閱讀等，有時候也可以跟別人聊聊自己喜歡的書、喜歡的作家。

會話1

例 Do you know this book?

你知道這本書嗎？

例 Of·course! She is my favorite writer!

當然啊，她是我最喜歡的作家！

會話2

例 This is really a good book.

這真是一本好書。

例 Were you reading this last time I saw you crying?

我上次看到你哭的時候你是不是在讀這本書啊？

 ∩track 140

那是我最愛的女/男演員

That is my favorite actress / actor.

解析

　　若是在聊電影、電視，也都會講到哪個演員很帥哪個演員很棒之類的，這時候就可以用到囉。

會話 1

例 Who is your favorite actress?
誰是你最喜歡的女演員？

例 I would say Meryl Streep.
應該是梅莉史翠普。

例 She is one of my favorites too!
她也是我最喜歡的女演員之一！

會話 2

例 Bruce Willis is my favorite actor.
布魯斯威利是我最喜歡的男演員。

例 Seriously? He's all washed-up.
真的嗎？他很過氣耶。

那是我最愛的歌手

That is my favorite singer.

解 析

也如同之前提過的作家、演員，現在講到歌手，就可以來聊聊關於歌手的事囉。

會話 1

例 Will you go to the concert of your favorite singer?

你會去你最喜歡的歌手的演唱會嗎？

例 I would love to! But the ticket is so expensive....

我超想的啊！可是票有點貴……

會話 2

例 I heard he is your favorite singer, so I got you his album.

我聽說他是你最愛的歌手，所以我送你他的專輯。

例 Thank you so much. You are so sweet.

真的很謝謝你，你人太好了。

週末到了我好興奮

I feel stoked about the weekend.

解析

Stoked 比較有一點俚語的感覺，可是為了什麼而感到興奮、熱情洋溢，都可以用這個字哦。

會話 1

例 Hey, what are you doing?

嘿，你在幹嘛？

例 I just got off from work. I feel stoked about the weekend.

我剛下班，週末到了我好興奮。

會話 2

例 I feel stoked about my summer vacation.

暑假到了我好開心。

例 Good for you. I still need to work.

真是太好了，但我還是得工作。

Chapter

9

交通工具搭乘

有點晚了

It is late.

解析

有時候必須離開一個場合的時候，就會提及時間有點晚，該回家了，這時就可用這句話。

會話 1

例 It is late.
有點晚了。

例 Yeah, we should go.
對啊，我們該走了。

會話 2

例 Do you really need to leave now?
你真的現在就要走了嗎？

例 I am afraid so. It is late.
我想是的，有點晚了。

我想我該回家了

I think I need to go home.

解析

我該回家了、我想回家了或是我必須回家,這些都是告別前會說的話。

會話1

例 I think I need to go home.

我想我該回家了。

例 It's early.

還早呢。

例 My mom keeps calling.

我媽一直打來。

會話2

例 I want to go home. I'm so tired.

我想要回家了,我好累哦。

例 Ok, be careful.

好的,小心點。

需要搭便車嗎？

Do you need a ride?

解析

若是自己有車，問別人需不需要順便搭便車的時候就可以這樣説囉！非常好用的一句話。

會話1

例 Do you need a ride?

你需要搭便車嗎？

例 No, it's ok. I can take a bus.

哦沒關係，我搭公車就行。

會話2

例 Do you need a ride? I am going to visit a friend near your house.

你需要搭便車嗎？我會去你家附近看朋友。

例 Sure, thank you.

好啊，謝謝。

你要怎麼回家？
How do you go home?

解析

每次送朋友回家之前都會問一下他要怎麼回家，是要搭計程車、公車、捷運還是有人會來接呢？了解一下也比較安全。

會話 1

例 How do you go home?
你要怎麼回家？

例 My brother will pick me up.
我哥會來載我。

會話 2

例 How do you go home?
你要怎麼回家？

例 I think I will take the metro.
我想我應該會搭捷運。

例 But it's so late.
都這麼晚了。

🎧 track 143

我該搭乘什麼交通工具？

What should I take?

解析

不管是要從陌生的地方回家，還是要去一個比較不熟的地方，如果不曉得該搭乘什麼交通工具比較方便，就會問一下比較清楚的人囉。

會話 1

例 I will meet you at Kimberly's house tomorrow morning.

明天早上金柏莉家見。

例 What should I take to get there?

我該搭什麼去那邊啊？

例 I think the metro is faster than the bus.

我覺得捷運應該比公車快。

會話 2

例 I need to go home now. Do you know what I should take?

我該回家了，你覺得搭什麼車比較好？

例 I'm not sure, let me check.

我不確定，我查一下。

請問公車站牌在哪？

Where is the bus stop?

解析

這句話是到哪裡都可以用的到，也可以把公車站牌換成捷運站，反正只要是要搭乘交通工具都可以靈活運用。

會話 1

例 Excuse me. Where is the bus stop?

不好意思，請問公車站牌在哪裡？

例 Go straight and turn right, it is just at the corner.

直走然後右轉，就在轉角。

會話 2

例 Do you know where the metro station is?

你知道捷運站在哪裡嗎？

I remember it's not far from here….

我記得離這裡不遠……

🎧 track 144

Do you know where the gate is?

解析

講到登機門想到的就是搭飛機囉，辦好所有手續之後就是要到登機門等待，可是有時候機場非常的大，找來找去都找不到，這時候就一定要問一下服務人員了！

會話 1

例 Do you know where gate 22 is?

你知道22號登機門在哪裡嗎？

例 You need to take a shuttle to get there.

你必須搭接駁車過去哦。

會話 2

例 I can't find my gate.

我找不到我的登機門。

例 I think they just changed your gate.
我想他們剛剛換了另一個登機門了。

你需要轉乘

You need to transfer.

解析

這裡講到的是「轉乘」transfer不管是搭飛
機轉機，還是先搭捷運再搭公車，只要是
有換交通工具，都可以使用這個字哦。

會話 1

例 Do you know how I can get to the zoo?
你知道我該怎麼到動物園嗎？

例 You need to transfer at this station.
你要在這站換車哦。

會話 2

例 Do you have a direct flight?
你是直飛嗎？

例 No, I need to transfer three times.
不是，我要轉三次機。

一路平安

Have a safe trip.

解析

遇到朋友家人要出門旅行的，都會祝對方
可以平平安安，這時候就可以這麼說囉！

會話 **1**

例 I'm leaving tomorrow.

我明天就要走囉。

例 Have a safe trip. I will miss you.

一路平安，我會想念你的。

會話 **2**

例 Have a safe flight.

飛行順利。

例 Thank you.

謝謝你。

小心點

Be careful.

解析

對每個人都可以這麼說，不管是去哪裡做什麼事，最重要的就是安全第一。

會話 1

例 Be careful when you go home late.
晚回家要小心點。

例 Ok, don't worry.
好，別擔心。

會話 2

例 Be careful. That place is not very safe.
小心點，那個地方不是很安全。

例 I will.
我會的。

我迷路了

I am lost.

解析

迷路了該怎麼說？需要朋友家人解救的時候，就可以說：我迷路了，我不知道我在哪裡！

會話1

例 Help me. I'm lost.

幫我，我迷路了。

例 How can I help you if you don't know where you are?

如果你不知道是什麼地方，我怎麼幫你啊？

會話2

例 Where are we?

我們在哪裡？

例 I think we are lost.

我想我們迷路了。

交通真是一團糟

The traffic is terrible.

解析

只要是在城市裡，一定會遇到難以避免的交通問題，很多時候都會提起交通的問題，另外塞車就是用 traffic jam 來表示囉。

會話 1

例 We can't drive.

我們不能開車。

例 Why?

為什麼？

例 It's 5pm, the traffic will be terrible.

下午五點，路上交通一定很糟糕。

會話 2

例 Why are you so late?

你怎麼遲到這麼久？

例 The traffic jam was a nightmare.

塞車真是個惡夢。

🎧 track 147

行李太重了

My luggage is overweight.

解析

重點是在說超重這件事，也就是 overweight，在搭飛機的時候最害怕會遇到的事之一就是行李超重了，因為超過的重量要付很貴的錢！

會話 1

例 What are you doing?

你在幹嘛？

例 My luggage is overweight. I need to take things out.

我的行李太重了，我需要拿些東西出來。

會話 2

例 Don't bring too many things; your luggage might be overweight.

別帶太多東西，有可能會超重哦。

例 What is the maximum weight of one suitcase?

一件行李最重是多少啊？

他們把我的行李搞丟了

They lost my luggage.

解析

出去玩還有一件最害怕的事就是行李不見！有時候不管有沒有轉機，航空公司就是有可能把行李搞丟，雖然大部份的時間都會找回來，不過也是一件另人受不了的事！

會話 1

例 They lost my luggage.

他們把我的行李搞丟了。

例 Not again!

不會吧，又來！

會話 2

例 This is the third time your airline has lost my luggage.

這是你們航空公司第三次把我的行李搞丟了。

例 We are sincerely sorry.

我們真的是非常抱歉。

 track 148

我會暈車

I get car sick.

解析

日常生活中不管去哪都少不了要坐車，暈車要怎麼說呢？

會話 1

例 I hate going through the mountains by car.

我很討厭開車上山。

例 I know you get car sick, but this is the only choice.

我知道你會暈車，但是我們沒有其它選擇了。

會話 2

例 I don't want to go. I get car sick.

我不想去，我會暈車。

例 Ok, that's too bad.

好吧，那太可惜了。

我不會開車

I don't know how to drive.

解 析

不會開車的人還是大有人在，所以除了説
這句之外，也可以説 I can't drive. 駕照就
是 driver's license.

會話 1

例 Do you drive?

你會開車嗎？

例 No, I don't. I don't know how to drive.

不會，我不會開車。

會話2

例 Do you have a driver's license?

你有駕照嗎？

例 Yes, I do.

我有啊。

例 But I never see you drive.

可是我從來沒看過你開車。

🎧track 149

你是一個好駕駛

You are a good driver.

解析

開車的駕駛也有分好與差，有的人開車你
會覺得很舒服很安全，有的人開車則是會
讓你膽顫心驚。

會話1

例 I think Tony is a very good driver.

我認為東尼是個好駕駛。

例 I agree.

我同意。

會話 2

例 We all agree that you are not a very good driver.

我們都同意你不是一個好駕駛。

例 Why?

為什麼？

例 Because you never put on your seat belt. That's really dangerous.

因為你從來不繫安全帶，那樣真的很危險。

酒後不開車

Don't drink and drive.

解析

酒後開車不僅非常危險，害己還會害到無辜的人，所以千千萬萬要記得，也要提醒他人不要酒後開車。

會話 1

例 You can't drive. You were drinking.

你不能開車，你喝酒了。

例 Just a little bit.

只有喝一點點啊。

例 Do not drink and drive. You might kill someone.

不行酒後開車，你會害死人的。

會話 2

例 I can't forgive those people who drive after drinking.

我不能原諒那些喝了酒還要開車的人。

例 Totally.

沒錯。

我的班機誤點了

My plane is delayed.

解析

飛機最常出現的狀況就是為了氣候問題而延後，有時候火車也會發生同樣的情形，這時候就可以這麼說囉。

會話 1

例 My plane is delayed.

我的班機誤點了。

例 For how long?

要等多久？

例 I don't know. Maybe one to two hours.

我不曉得，也是一至二個小時吧。

會話 2

例 I'm calling to tell you my train is delayed because of the typhoon.

我打來是跟你說我的火車因為颱風所以誤點了。

例 Ok, I got it.

好的，知道了。

火車站見

I will meet you at the train station.

解析

出去玩常常都會約在大地標見面，最常約的就是交通站，像是捷運站、火車站或是一些很大的地標，這時候就可以這樣使用囉。

會話1

例 I will meet you at the train station.

我跟你約火車站見。

例 Is there only one exit?

只有一個出口嗎？

會話2

例 I will meet you at the MRT museum station.

我跟你約在博物館站見。

例 Ok, no problem.

好的，沒問題。

🎧track 151

叫車比較安全

It's safer to call a cab.

解析

搭計程車最擔心的就是個人安全問題，尤其是女孩了深夜搭車的話最好是叫車會比較放心哦。

會話 1

例 I will take a cab home.

我會搭計程車回家。

例 Let me call a cab for you.

我幫你叫車。

會話 2

例 It's safer to call a cab.

叫車比較安全。

例 Yeah, you're right.

你說的沒錯。

3
4
6

到…接我

Pick me up at….

解析

Pick someone up 就是接某人的意思，這句話也非常實用，因為告訴對方要到哪裡接人就是這樣説囉。

會話1

例 Can you pick me up at the front gate of my school?

你可以到學校大門口接我嗎？

例 Sure, but you might have to wait for 5 minutes.

好的，可是你要等我五分鐘哦。

會話2

例 Where should I pick you up?

我要到哪裡接你？

例 I will be at home. Pick me up at my house.

我會在家，所以來我家接我吧。

永續圖書
線上購物網

www.foreverbooks.com.tw

- ◆ 加入會員即享活動及會員折扣。
- ◆ 每月均有優惠活動，期期不同。
- ◆ 新加入會員三天內訂購書籍不限本數金額，
  即贈送精選書籍一本。（依網站標示為主）

專業圖書發行、書局經銷、圖書出版

永續圖書總代理：
五觀藝術出版社、培育文化、棋茵出版社、大拓文化、讀
品文化、雅典文化、知音人文化、手藝家出版社、璟申文
化、智學堂文化、語言鳥文化

活動期內，永續圖書將保留變更或終止該活動之權利及最終決定權。

馬上說，生活英文迷你短句

雅致風靡　典藏文化

親愛的顧客您好，感謝您購買這本書。即日起，填寫讀者回函卡寄回至本公司，我們每月將抽出一百名回函讀者，寄出精美禮物並享有生日當月購書優惠！想知道更多更即時的消息，歡迎加入"永續圖書粉絲團"您也可以選擇傳真、掃描或用本公司準備的免郵回函寄回，謝謝。

傳真電話：（02）8647-3660　　　　電子信箱：yungjiuh@ms45.hinet.net

姓名：		性別：	□男　□女
出生日期：　年　　月　　日		電話：	
學歷：		職業：	
E-mail：			
地址：□□□			
從何處購買此書：		購買金額：　　　　元	

購買本書動機：□封面 □書名 □排版 □內容 □作者 □偶然衝動

你對本書的意見：
內容：□滿意□尚可□待改進　　編輯：□滿意□尚可□待改進
封面：□滿意□尚可□待改進　　定價：□滿意□尚可□待改進

其他建議：

總經銷：永續圖書有限公司

永續圖書線上購物網
www.foreverbooks.com.tw

您可以使用以下方式將回函寄回。

您的回覆，是我們進步的最大動力，謝謝。

① 使用本公司準備的免郵回函寄回。

② 傳真電話：（02）8647-3660

③ 掃描圖檔寄到電子信箱：

yungjiuh@ms45.hinet.net

沿此線對折後寄回，謝謝。

廣 告 回 信

基隆郵局登記證

基隆廣字第056號

雅致風靡　典藏文化